FROM ENEMY'S DAUGHTER TO EXPECTANT BRIDE

—

OLIVIA GATES

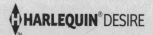

HARLEQUIN® DESIRE

Recycling programs
for this product may
not exist in your area.

ISBN-13: 978-0-373-73350-7

From Enemy's Daughter to Expectant Bride

Printed in U.S.A.

He took her into the ballroom so they'd conclude this business with her boss, and he could have her all to himself again.

Eliana spooled away from him, flashing him an exquisite smile. "I'll go finish my own mission."

Before he could stop her, an erratic movement caught his eye.

Ferreira.

Rafael's enemy was on a collision course with them.

Before any of them could move, Ferreira was pulling Eliana into his arms.

Aggression erupted, almost bursting Rafael's head. *He* was her boss? And he was on hugging terms with her?

Then the words Ferreira kept saying as he clutched Eliana sank into Rafael's mind.

Ellie, my baby girl, you're okay.

Rafael stared at the woman he'd lost his mind over, in the arms of the man he was here to destroy.

And everything crashed into place.

* * *

From Enemy's Daughter to Expectant Bride is part of The Billionaires of Black Castle series: Only their dark pasts could lead these men to the light of true love.

* * *

If you're on Twitter,
tell us what you think of Harlequin Desire!
#harlequindesire

Dear Reader,

The Billionaires of Black Castle series idea came to me years ago. A blood brotherhood forged in the darkest of pasts who'd escaped the shadow organization who'd kidnapped them as children and made them into unstoppable mercenaries. But I didn't know if I could write such a series for the Harlequin Desire line.

When I finally approached my wonderful editor, Stacy Boyd, she loved the idea of those larger-than-life billionaires, each from a different ethnic background, with their adventures and love stories spanning the world, from Brazil to Japan to Russia to desert and Mediterranean kingdoms.

So was born this series, taking place ten years after their escape, with their secrets deeply buried and their new identities as top world movers and shakers through their joint globe-spanning business Black Castle Enterprises.

But those men won't just sit back and enjoy their phenomenal success and power. They won't rest until they fulfill their blood oath to reclaim their heritages, right the wrongs that had been dealt them, and bring down those who'd imprisoned and exploited them. And as each embarks on his own quest, the last thing he believes can happen is for love to stand in the way of what he wants most, or the mission he's sworn to with his brothers.

And that's just what happens to Rafael Moreno Salazar, this book's hero. He's finally about to enact his revenge on the man who'd sold him into slavery...when Eliana explodes into his life. It is only after he's overwhelmed by desire for her that he finds out she's his enemy's daughter.

What follows is a roller coaster of passion, emotions and angst. I so hope you enjoy reading as much as I enjoyed writing it!

Thanks for reading!

Olivia Gates

Books by Olivia Gates

Harlequin Desire

Other titles by this author
available in ebook format.

Silhouette Desire

OLIVIA GATES

has always pursued creative passions such as singing and handicrafts. She still does, but only one of her passions grew gratifying enough, consuming enough, to become an ongoing career—writing.

She is most fulfilled when she is creating worlds and conflicts for her characters, then exploring and untangling them bit by bit, sharing her protagonists' every heart-wrenching heartache and hope, their every heart-pounding doubt and trial, until she leads them to an indisputably earned and gloriously satisfying happy ending.

When she's not writing, she is a doctor, a wife to her own alpha male and a mother to one brilliant girl and one demanding Angora cat. Visit Olivia at www.oliviagates.com.

To Pat Cooper. I'm so honored and grateful my writing has struck such a chord within you. Your reviews have literally changed my life.

Prologue

He woke up in darkness again.

His cheeks were wet, his heart battering his chest, and his screams for his mother and father still shredding his throat.

"Get up, Numbers."

The vicious voice had terror expanding in his chest. The first time he'd heard it, he'd been terrified, thinking it was a stranger in his bedroom. But he'd soon realized it had been even worse. He'd no longer been at home, but somewhere narrow and long with no windows and no furniture. He'd been on the freezing ground, hands tied behind his back. That voice speaking heavily accented English, the language he knew so well, had said the same thing then.

And that had been how this nightmare had started.

"Seems Numbers wants another beating."

That was the other man. He believed he'd never see anyone but these scary men ever again. And they called him Numbers. It was why they'd taken him. Because he was good with numbers.

He'd been offended when they'd first said that about him. He wasn't "good with numbers." He was a mathematical prodigy. That was what his parents and teachers and all the experts who'd sought him had said he was.

He'd corrected them, and he'd gotten his first ever slap for it. It had almost snapped his neck, sending him crashing into the wall. As the shock and pain had registered, he'd realized that this was real. He was no longer safe and protected. Anything could and would be done to him.

At first, that had made him angry. He'd said if they returned him to his parents, he wouldn't tell them they'd dared lay a hand on him. The two men had laughed, just like he'd always imagined devils would. One had told the other that this Numbers kid might take longer to break than they'd thought.

He'd still insisted his name wasn't Numbers, and the other man had backhanded him on his other cheek, even more viciously.

As he'd lain on the ground, shaking with fear and helplessness, the men had told him what to expect from now on.

"You'll never see your parents or leave this place again. You now belong to us. If you do everything we tell you, the moment we tell you, then you won't be punished. Not too bad."

But he'd disobeyed their every order ever since, no matter how severely they'd punished him for it. He'd hoped they'd give up on him and send him home. But they'd only grown more brutal, seemed to be enjoying hurting and humiliating him more, and the hope that this nightmare might end had kept dwindling.

"Shall we give Numbers a choice of punishments today?"

He heard his tormentors snickering, could barely see their silhouettes towering over him out of the eye that wasn't swollen shut. And in that moment, he gave up.

It finally sank in that what he'd endured their abuse so long for would never happen.

This nightmare would never end.

His captors would never stop their cruelty, his parents would never rescue him and no one else would ever help him. It would never stop getting worse.

And if this was what his life would be like from now on, he no longer wanted to live.

But he couldn't even kill himself. All he had in his cell were metal bowls for dirty water and slimy gunk and the bucket he used for a toilet. There was no way to escape them even through death. Except maybe...

The idea took hold in a second. He'd tried everything except playing along. Maybe if he did, they'd think they'd broken him, and let him out of his cell. He could escape then.

Or die trying.

One of the giants kicked him in the ribs. "Up, Numbers."

Gritting his teeth against the shriek of pain, he rose.

A terrible laugh. "Numbers finally obeys."

"Let's see if he really does." The other monster shoved his foul-breathed face in his. "What's your name, boy?"

The burning liquid in his shriveled stomach rose to his mouth. He swallowed it with the last thought of resistance. "Numbers."

A slap stung across his sore cheek, if not as hard as usual. They'd punish him anyway, just not as badly when he obeyed. "And why are you here?"

"Because I'm good with numbers."

"And what will you do?"

"Everything you say." Another slap left his ears ringing, his head spinning, yet he continued, "The moment you say it."

In the faint light coming from outside, he saw them exchange smiles of malicious satisfaction. They believed they'd succeeded in breaking him. And they had. But he didn't intend to live long enough for them to enjoy their victory.

And they did as he'd thought they would—they dragged him out of his cell. Too weak to walk, he hung between them, his bare feet and the knees exposed through his tattered pants scraping on the cold, cobbled ground.

Barely able to raise his head to look where they were taking him, he got glimpses of soaring, blackened columns and arches, with a roiling gray sky between them. The whole place looked like a medieval fortress from one of the video games his father had gotten him. The one thing he noticed or cared about now was that the walls between the columns were low enough to jump over. To escape…or fall to his death.

Then one of the monsters said, "If you get near the walls, you'll get caught, beaten then thrown back in your cell for twice as long as it took to break you the first time."

So even *that* plan was impossible. But he couldn't go on like this anymore. He couldn't take it.

Before he begged them to just kill him and be done with it, they pulled open two towering wooden doors, dragged him across the threshold and hurled him to the rough ground.

When he finally managed to raise his head, he saw that they were in a huge hall with rows of tables filled with silent boys who'd all turned at their entrance.

"This worm is your newest addition. If you see him doing anything you're not allowed, report him. You'll have a bonus."

With that, his two jailers turned and left him on his knees facing the boys. His pride surged back under their scrutiny, had him staggering to his feet, the initial hope he'd felt when he'd realized he wasn't alone here draining away. He knew boys could be cruel to those smaller and weaker.

And from a first sweep around the room, he was probably the youngest around.

He stood, trying not to hug his aching side, not to show weakness, and almost sagged back to his knees in relief as they turned back to their food and whispered conversations.

So they were all afraid to even raise their voices as the boys in his old school had, who'd been free to laugh and joke. These boys were prisoners like him. They'd been broken before him.

Painfully good smells of hot food hit him, making him dizzier with hunger. Trying to appear steady, he headed toward the source of the aromas.

He was struggling to reach the lid of one of the massive containers when a hand raised it. He hadn't felt its owner's approach.

It was an older boy with a shaved head and piercing black eyes who was already as tall as his own father. But instead of being intimidated by the boy's size and fierce looks, he felt…reassured by his presence.

"My name is Phantom. What's yours?"

His real name rose to his tongue before he swallowed it. This boy might be waiting for him to do something "they weren't allowed to," like tell his real name, so he could report him and get a bonus.

To be on the safe side, he only said, "Numbers."

The boy's winged black eyebrows rose. "That's your specialty? But you can't be older than seven."

"I'm eight."

At his indignation, the boy's gaze gentled. "The first month—or three in your case—of starvation made us all look smaller. You must now eat well, so you can grow as big and strong as possible."

"Like you?"

Phantom's lips twitched. "I'm not done growing. But I'm working on it."

The older boy filled a bowl of steaming stew that smelled mouthwatering compared to the rotting messes he'd been unable to force down for what he'd just now realized had been the past three months. He'd had no way of knowing how long it had been until Phantom had told him.

After handing it over, Phantom filled himself a bowl, then beckoned for him to follow. "If you warranted a name according to your skill that young, you must be a prodigy."

It pleased him intensely that this huge boy with the soundless steps and penetrating eyes could see him for what he was. Even after his jailers had stripped him of everything that made him himself.

Encouraged, he asked, "How old are you?"

"Fifteen. I've been here since I was four."

The boy had answered his next question before he'd asked it, telling him that what his jailers had said was true.

He'd never leave here.

They reached one of the tables and Phantom gestured for him to sit down. There were five other boys, each looking as different as could be from the other, all older than him, but none as old as Phantom.

Two boys scooted along the bench to make space for him as Phantom introduced him to them, his lips somehow not moving, so it would appear to the guards who flanked the hall that he wasn't talking at all. Each of the boys introduced himself. Lightning, Bones, Cypher, Brainiac and Wildcard.

As they continued to eat, each of them asked him something, about his past life. He emulated the boys in stealth, telling them truths without revealing facts. Then they started giving him equations, which he solved with perfect accuracy no matter how convoluted they made them.

By the time they finished eating, he felt he'd known these boys for a long time. But the guards were announcing the end of the meal, and all the boys stood up to leave the hall.

Unable to control his anxiety, he clung to Phantom's arm. "Will I see you again?"

Phantom gave him a stern look, making him remove his hand before the guards noticed. But his voice was gentle when he said, "I'll see that you're brought to our ward."

"You can do that?"

"There's a lot you can do around here, if you know how."

"Will you teach me?"

Phantom raised his eyes to the other boys. And it was then he realized they weren't just fellow prisoners who sat together for meals or shared the same ward. These boys were a team. And Phantom was asking their approval before he let him join them.

Suddenly, this was all he wanted in life. To be part of their team. His old life was gone. And he just knew he wouldn't have a new one without these boys.

He watched each boy give Phantom a slight nod, each filling him with hope he'd thought forever dead.

Before Phantom started walking away, leaving him behind, he said, "Welcome to our brotherhood, Numbers. And to Black Castle."

One

Rafael Moreno Salazar stood in the shadows, looking down from the mezzanine of his newly acquired mansion in Rio de Janeiro.

The grand ball was in full swing. All the major names in the marketing world were enjoying his exclusive hors d'oeuvres and free-flowing Moët et Chandon and waltzing to the elegant music of his live orchestra. And he hadn't yet made an appearance.

He was leaving his guests to…stew, letting their curiosity about him and his intentions reach a fever pitch.

He'd been doing that since his announcement. That Rafael Salazar—the enigma who'd revolutionized financial technologies—was shopping for a marketing partner in the Western hemisphere. Although the announcement's impact was already huge, he'd kept stoking interest by deepening his mystery. Then he'd added a pinch of spice. A handful of dirt, really.

As he always did with potential clients and associates, he'd let info leak that his background was in organized crime. As it was. Just not in the way people imagined. He and his brothers had had their own shadow operation in their beginnings.

Heads of state had been fascinated by his avant-garde methods from the start, but they hadn't courted him aggressively except when they'd found out those methods had been forged in the crucible of crime and tested through the ingeniousness of corruption.

But he hadn't been sure the marketing tycoons he was baiting would be as open to dealing with someone who dabbled in the world's grayest zones and was one of those zones' most ambiguous figures.

But instead of being repelled, it seemed everyone thought any illegal skills and liaisons he commanded would make him an even more lucrative partner. And if he was as formidable as it was rumored, he'd also be invulnerable. They could all do with a partner bullets bounced off.

And there they were, the hopeful candidates, pretending to be enjoying his lavish party and trying to be gracious to one another. But he could feel them seething with frustration, wondering whom he'd favor if and when he finally deigned to grace his own ball.

"Will you finally make an appearance tonight, Numbers?"

He slanted a calm glance at the man who'd appeared silently at his side. "I just might this time, Cobra."

The Englishman he'd called Cobra for the past twenty years curled a ruthless lip as he examined the scene. Rafael had told him the same thing on three previous occasions.

To the world, he was Richard Graves—the name he'd picked when they'd manufactured their new identities. At forty-two, Richard looked like a Hollywood movie star, and at first glance, he could pass for Rafael's older brother. They had almost the same build and coloring, only Richard's jet-black hair was threaded with discreet silver. On closer inspection, however, their bone structure revealed their different ethnicities, with Rafael being of Portuguese Brazilian stock.

But there was one other major difference between them, and it wasn't on the surface. It was in their specialties.

Though Rafael had been trained to be deadly, his main power lay in his mind. He'd rarely relied on his prowess in violence but was the go-to guy to liquidate targets financially. Richard was code-named Cobra for the best reasons. He was the total package of lethality. His liquidations had always been the literal kind. He now hid the deadliness that made him the ultimate assassin behind a facade of refinement. Until you examined him. Or he examined you. Rafael didn't know any mere mortals who could withstand his scrutiny.

But Richard's days of eradicating scum were behind him. Or so he said. But whether this was true or not, he now eliminated threats in the worlds of business and politics with an equally ruthless precision. With Richard as his partner and protector, Rafael felt confident that the past would never catch up with him…and that the future could hold no worries.

Richard pulled back, leveled probing eyes on him. "Aren't you playing this with too much deliberation? You waited years to concoct this plan—I thought you'd be a bit more eager to finally put it into action."

Rafael jerked one shoulder. "I'm in no hurry."

"Really? Could have fooled me." Richard huffed. "Seriously, all you've done for two months is set up such events, then stand in the wings watching. Don't you think you've done enough reconnaissance?"

"After twenty-four years, you think two months is too long for me to savor the anticipation of my revenge?"

"Put that way, no." Richard made a sound of self-deprecation. "Seems I'm the one who can't contain my impatience. You've always been the most methodical, *patient* person I know. That is, along with your dear, relentless Phantom. But you still have one up on him. On anyone. You see the intricacies of probability as simple equations when they're a maze to the rest of us."

Rafael didn't contradict him. He'd long known that the fluke of his mathematical ability did make him see the world in a different way.

But no matter what he'd just claimed, Richard was as clear-sighted as he was in his own way when it came to his concerns. However, when it came to Rafael's, Richard had zero tolerance. He'd killed for him, would no doubt do so again if need be. He'd die for him. The feeling was absolutely mutual.

It never stopped amazing him that he'd not only been blessed with such a "brother" but with seven. Even though they were down to six these days.

Shaking away the disturbing memory of how they'd lost Cypher, seemingly forever, he sighed. "Maybe I'm discovering revenge is a dish best served cold."

At Richard's unconvinced grunt, Rafael chuckled, then sipped his champagne, swirling the sweet taste of vicious expectation.

His revenge *would* be cold. As bitterly cold as the prison he'd grown up in. As agonizingly slow as time had sheared past there. As grimly inexorable as the hatred he'd nursed all those years for those who'd had a hand in his enslavement.

Twelve interminable years of enduring his enslavers' dehumanizing as they'd molded him into the mercenary the Organization would later lease to the highest bidders. Their patrons ranged from top names in politics and commerce to those in organized crime, espionage and war mongering.

He'd been one of a few hundred boys, picked from all over the world. Some kidnapped from their families, others bought or bartered, many more plucked from orphanages, the streets or chaos-torn zones. They'd all been way above average, physically and mentally. Some were gifted. Like him and his brothers.

The Organization's "recruiters" chose their potential operatives using unerring criteria, and they went to great lengths to "acquire" them. They delivered them to that prison in the depths of the Balkans, where they were kept segregated from the world in that sinister fortress his brothers had named Black Castle.

The Organization acquired children as young as possible, the easier to shape them. The ones they acquired a bit older, like him, or younger but strong enough to resist, like his brothers, they broke first, before they put them in training.

Training was a euphemism for the hell, both physical and psychological, that they put them through to forge them into lethal weapons. Once they graduated to fieldwork, they were sent out in teams according to the skill set each mission required. They performed under the airtight surveillance of their "handlers." Death rewarded any attempt to escape.

Yet he'd survived escaping and, before that, the years of oppression and abuse. Not that it had been because of his own strength. He'd had none left after that first period of isolation and torture. If he hadn't met his brothers, he wouldn't have lasted much longer. Then, four years later, Richard had taken him under his wing, too. Richard and his brothers had saved his sanity, and his life.

Phantom, now Numair Al Aswad, had fulfilled the promise he'd made that day in the dining hall when he and the boys had recognized him as a kindred spirit. From that point on, they'd made life worth living, their brotherhood replacing the family he'd lost. After proving himself worthy of their total trust, they'd included him in the blood pact they'd sworn. That they'd one day escape and become powerful enough to bring the entire Organization down.

To that end, Phantom had maneuvered the Organization into constantly teaming them up together until they became their prized strike force. This inseparable unit had been vital to their very long-term plans.

Phantom had also made them believe they'd eradicated their individuality, had turned them into inhuman weapons to be pointed wherever they pleased.

Once they'd become trusted and depended on, they'd been granted more autonomy, until that laxness had allowed them to execute their escape.

When they'd finally broken out, they'd gone deep underground, using their combined covert expertise to forge new identities....

"Reminiscing?"

Richard, his onetime handler, always read him with uncanny accuracy. It was how he'd found Rafael and the others after they'd escaped—by tracing him.

His brothers' handlers had thankfully had no insight into their true nature. But since Richard had been assigned to him when he'd been twelve, an unbreakable bond had developed between them. Richard, ice-cold and implicitly trusted by the Organization, had hidden it perfectly. But there'd been no hiding anything from his brothers. Especially from Phantom and Cypher. Those two saw *everything*. And seeing his growing rapport with Richard had made them more apprehensive by the day. Their trepidation had proved wellfounded when Richard had found them.

They'd distrusted Richard as totally as Rafael trusted him, considered him one of their enslavers. Their decision had been unanimous. Richard had to die.

Rafael hadn't known whom to fear for more. Richard was

the most lethal operative the Organization had ever had and certainly capable of wiping them all out. There'd been only one way he could avert that catastrophic situation.

He'd declared he'd stake his life on both sides, so if there was any killing, they had to kill him, too. Thankfully, they'd trusted him and his judgment implicitly, and it had been enough to make them all back down.

Yet even after he'd proved their escape plans wouldn't have worked without Richard's covert help, they'd still suspected Richard's motives. It had taken proof that Richard had been a hostage of the Organization himself for them to believe that he wanted to bring them down, too.

It had still taken his brothers ages to warm up to Richard. Never in Numair's case. Rafael remained the link between them, since he didn't relish tearing Richard and Numair's fangs out of each other's flesh.

Those two had never had a truce, not even while they'd collated their unique skills to guide their brotherhood into building their joint enterprise. The one thing they'd ever agreed on was the name of their business—the name they'd given their prison, where they and their brotherhood had been forged. And so Black Castle Enterprises had been born.

Their business now spanned the world, with each becoming a billionaire in his own right. Each was also on a personal quest. Some searching for the family they'd been taken from, others for the heritage they'd been stripped of, some for a new purpose in life. But beyond planning the Organization's downfall to save other children from their same fate, they had one more quest in common. Investigating how they'd ended up in the hands of the Organization.

Rafael had recently found out exactly how.

"Ferreira is down there?"

Richard's question brought him out of his musings. "Of course."

"So when will you put the man out of his misery?"

Rafael glanced fondly at his friend. "I wouldn't put it past you to mean that literally."

Richard gave him his patented predatory smile. "Oh, no. I think your plan is a much worse fate. I couldn't have thought of a more diabolical one."

"High praise from the man who puts 007 to shame."

Not one for false modesty, Richard only said, "You know I'm a fan of subtle and protracted torture."

Indeed. And his impending torment of Ferreira would have an abundance of both elements. Disgracing him and oh-so-gradually stripping him of his wealth would only be the beginning.

"Your plot is far more effective than putting a bullet in his brain. I just wish you'd get on with it."

"So you no longer disapprove of my direct approach?"

Richard shrugged. "A remote one remains better. It would be the perfect setup if he didn't realize where the blows were coming from. But that's logic talking. And there's more than logic involved here. You need the satisfaction of looking that git in the eyes as you stick the knife in and turn it."

Richard had originally advised against getting close to Ferreira, with the inherent drawbacks and dangers that entailed. It now warmed Rafael that his friend not only understood his need, he empathized. He wanted this for him. This gratification. This closure.

And he would come close. He'd make Ferreira taste everything he'd ever hungered for…before snatching it away. Rafael would have a front-row seat to his betrayal and desperation.

Putting his glass down, he sighed. "But you're right. It's time I got that satisfaction. I won't single Ferreira out tonight, though. I'll dangle myself, pretend to take pitches, let the mystery around me build a bit more, before…"

Something sizzled at the back of his neck. As if a soft hand stroked him there, or a hot breath blew over his skin.

Frowning, he turned to investigate the source of the disturbance. It couldn't be someone's gaze. He wasn't in anyone's line of sight.

As expected, no one was looking his way. But those sensations only increased, enveloped his body and...

Everything seemed to fade as his senses converged on the beacon of disruption. A woman.

Framed in the ballroom's doorway, she stood as if at a loss for what to do. She was swathed in an ethereal off-the-shoulder cream evening gown, gleaming hair swept away from a face that seemed almost unreal before cascading to a tiny waist that...

"Before what?"

He blinked Richard's question away, resuming his focus on her. Though he'd never suffered anything like this before, he knew what it was. A bolt of attraction. More than that. Recognition...of the woman who translated his every fantasy into glorious reality.

He had to be imagining this. But all his senses told him he wasn't. This felt real.

One way to find out. Get closer....

"What are you staring at, Numbers?"

This time Richard's intrusion annoyed him. He realized his reaction was exaggerated, but he didn't want to talk, couldn't risk shattering this moment.

As if afraid he'd startle her out of her indecision, which afforded him the leisure to examine her, he whispered, "Her."

Richard stepped forward. "Who? That woman at the door?"

Surprised, he turned to him. "You see her?"

Richard scowled. "You asleep on your feet again?"

He hadn't slept in over twenty-four hours, but that had nothing to do with his reaction to her. "I'm wide-awake.

Though she does belong in a dream. She looks like she's just stepped out of a fairy tale."

Richard's incredulity surpassed his. "You're serious?"

"I am. I…"

His thoughts stalled. She'd started walking into the ballroom, but her uncertain steps, her darting eyes and the way she fiddled with the long chain of her purse revealed her discomfort. Everything about her unconscious grace and reluctant demeanor made something rev behind his sternum. It intensified with her every step until he had to rub the heel of his hand against it.

"How could this be real?"

"It isn't."

Richard's response startled him. He hadn't realized he'd spoken out loud. "How can you say that?"

"I can because she's just another pretty blonde."

He looked at his friend as if he'd grown a third eye. "She's *not* blonde. Are you even talking about the same woman?"

Richard seemed about to argue, then changed his mind. "Whatever. Just go initiate your incursion."

"It won't be an incursion. I will approach her with utmost finesse."

Richard frowned. "I'm talking about Ferreira."

"Forget Ferreira. I'll…"

Rafael stopped as he realized something. He *couldn't* approach her. He'd been scrupulous about keeping any photos of himself out of the media. But if anyone knew what he looked like, they were down there at the ball. He didn't want to risk anyone recognizing him, not now that he'd decided against making an appearance. This evening had suddenly become all about establishing contact with this magical being.

He turned to Richard. "Cobra, bring her to me."

His former handler blinked. "What's wrong with you,

Numbers? You've never reacted to a woman like this before."

"She's not just 'a woman.'"

Richard snorted. "Oh, yes, that's right. She just slithered out of a fairy tale."

Rafael gritted his teeth, impatience shooting through him. "Just go down and get her up here."

"You want me—the man famed for putting people at *such* ease—to approach a woman I don't know and command her to come with me…to meet another man she doesn't know? A man who currently looks deranged? You expect this fairy being to be a total moron, too?"

Richard's derision tripped some still functioning logic circuits. That scenario did seem implausible.

But he *had* to get that woman alone.

Suddenly, another idea came to him. "I'll go down with you and stand outside the ballroom. You just get her to me. I'll take it from there."

"I'm your protector, not your pimp, Numbers."

"Oh, shut up. And move it."

With one last glance as if to a madman, Richard turned and headed downstairs. Rafael dogged his steps, scenarios crowding in his overheated imagination.

What if this excitement fizzled out once he saw her up close? Worse, what if it didn't…but she didn't reciprocate it? Or what if she *was* interested, but like all other women, her attraction was based purely on his looks, wealth and power? Worst of all, what if she was already taken?

No. This last possibility he categorically rejected.

She wasn't taken. He just knew it.

At the edge of the ballroom, Richard looked back as if hoping he'd come to his senses. Rafael only shoved him forward.

Grunting a curse, Richard walked away, cutting through

the crowd. At six foot six, he towered a head above everyone, making it easy for Rafael to monitor his progress.

Then he saw her. Pressing to the periphery, as if taking refuge from the crowd, wishing she were anywhere but there.

Everything inside him tightened, anticipating the moment Richard pointed her in his direction. Or something. He had no idea what his friend would do or say to get her to cross the ballroom to meet him.

Richard was feet away from her when she suddenly turned her elegant head. And looked straight into *his* eyes.

A bolt hit him through the heart. A growl escaped his lips as the current forked within him. Then again as her eyes widened and her tense features went slack.

He wasn't imagining this. She'd felt his focus, and it had made her home in on him, even across the distance and with him in shadows. He'd had the same effect on her.

And without volition, holding her mesmerized gaze, he raised his hand and…beckoned.

Her stare faltered, her throat worked. Peach stained her chiseled cheekbones and her gaze darted around, as if unable to believe she was his target.

Look back. Look back at me.

As if against her will, her eyes dragged back to his.

Satisfaction surged through him. She'd felt his need and had been unable to resist it. Testing his theory, he beckoned again, taking a step backward deeper into the shadows.

She stepped forward, looking surprised, as if she hadn't intended to move. He took another step back. She once again moved in his direction, the confusion on her exquisite face deepening. This live wire of attraction that had sprung to life between them *was* reeling her in to him. He hadn't needed Richard's help after all.

The steely Englishman glared down at her as she bypassed him in a daze. Realizing his mediation was no longer needed, he shook his head in exasperation and strode away. Richard fell off Rafael's radar as he focused on the vision he held in thrall, just as she held him. He continued to recede and beckon, drawing her toward him.

It took forever for her to weave through the throngs of people who turned to stare at her trancelike advance. Then at last, *at last,* she entered the deserted corridor. He took her deeper into his home where no one would come. She kept advancing after he stopped. Lips parted, eyes wide, face tilted up, she finally halted within arm's reach. The sconces illuminated her face and figure in golden radiance and soft shadow.

She was more than he'd thought from afar, her impact on him fiercer up close.

And she most definitely wasn't blond. Such a mundane word didn't describe her cascade of spun silk with its thousand shades. Each strand had the tones of Rio's beaches, its Sugarloaf Mountain and its sunrays at every time of day.

In contrast, her skin, from forehead to fingertips, was flawless cream. As for her body, it was *the* body sculpted to his every requirement, to accommodate his every desire and demand. At once willowy and womanly, unconscious femininity screamed in its every line and swell and curve.

Richard had been wrong about something else, too. She wasn't pretty. Or beautiful. She transcended such descriptions. From the intelligent forehead to the elegant nose to the lush lips, her face was a tapestry of perfections, embodying his every taste and fantasy. But it was her eyes, where her essence resided, that snared him. Wide, heavily fringed, a magnificent shape and slant, he'd thought he'd imagined their color as she'd approached. He hadn't. They were an intense, luminous tawny. The hue of fire. And just as dangerous.

But *her* effect wasn't about her physical attributes. Something about her just made him want to...devour her. He'd never been so ferociously attracted, or aroused. It was incomprehensible, but all he wanted was to unwrap her then bury himself inside her.

Even in his state, he realized that course of action wasn't advisable. Even if she was willing. Which, from her glazed stare and agitated breathing, she probably was.

"Obrigado, minha beleza."

He heard his hungry rasp, thanking her, calling her *his beauty* in his mother tongue. Though most of tonight's guests weren't Brazilian, he had a feeling she'd understand. And though he only thought in Portuguese and hadn't spoken it since he'd been abducted, it felt the only language personal enough, intimate enough, to do this moment justice.

"Wh-what for?"

His breath caught. She *had* understood, yet answered in English. Cultured, American English. And she sounded as shaken as she looked. Her voice was a soft, sultry caress, made to moan enchantments in his ear, against his flesh, in long, pleasure-drenched nights.

"For coming when I summoned you."

She blinked, as if emerging from a trance. "Summoned me?"

She obviously took exception to his choice of words. He wanted to tease her, say that she *had* obeyed his summons. But he couldn't talk—he needed to make that first contact. Holding her gaze, he reached out and cupped her cheek.

His breath hissed out as her flesh filled his palm, as he absorbed its texture and heat. She trembled in his grasp, pouring molten steel into his erection. Then her eyes darkened into burning coals and singed away his control.

Two urgent, stumbling steps had her back to the wall, plastering her between its unyielding barrier and his. Hot resilience cushioned his aching hardness and ripped a rumble from his gut. Her echoing gasp filled his lungs with her scent. A hint of jasmine, a mist of pheromones, a gust of compulsion. Hunger writhed inside him until he could no longer bear not tasting her.

Holding her stunned eyes with his, he hovered over her trembling lips for one last anticipation-laced moment. Then he obliterated the distance between them.

A spark arced between their lips, making him jerk up. Her eyes displayed shock, too; her lips trembled with it. But the rise and fall of her breasts was that of excitement, not distress. Then arousal seeped into her eyes, weighing down her lids, and made her lips swell, as if he'd already ravished them.

She wanted this. Wanted him. Like he wanted her.

And he didn't want just a kiss anymore. He wanted everything.

They'd exchanged two sentences—phrases—and he knew nothing about her. But this would follow no rules. The passion that had exploded into existence between them obliterated any.

He would take her first. As she wanted him to. Everything else would come later. Satisfying this overpowering hunger was the most important thing now. The only thing that mattered.

He bent, swept her up in his arms. She only gasped and went limp against him, her eyes enormous orbs of surrender.

Triumph and elation fueled his strides to his study. Kicking the door shut, he put her back on her feet and pressed her against it. Her feverish eyes assured him this was exactly what she wanted. Everything with him. Now.

"Sim, beleza, sim...tudo comigo...agora."

And he crashed his lips on hers.

propriate," then driven to that mansion in Armação dos Búzios, the "Hamptons of Brazil." The damn place was over two hours away. And she'd been lost an extra half hour before finding it.

After she finally did at six o'clock, she had memories of valet parking and walking through the ingeniously landscaped, multilevel gardens into the splendid, four-level edifice sprawling over what she thought was no less than ten thousand square feet. Outside, each spray of indirect illumination enhanced every white-painted arch, column and molding in its neo-Renaissance architecture, giving it the grandeur of a temple or cathedral. Inside, the pervasive, festive lighting came from an abundance of all-crystal chandeliers and antique brass *lampadaires,* giving the Portuguese-French–style gilded interior the feel of a fairy tale. Then she'd reached the ballroom, which was right out of one.

She remembered pausing at the threshold, wrestling with her dislike for crowds, then finally walking in since braving it was preferable to being subjected to more pleading.

Then as she'd kept to the periphery, avoiding the forced gaiety, she'd felt as if she was hit by lightning. Her eyes had jerked to the bolt's origin. And she'd met his gaze.

As her heart had stumbled like a horse on ice, he'd raised a hand made of elegance and power, and beckoned.

Breath hitching, she'd looked around to see who he was beckoning to. Once sure he was actually motioning to her, she'd had no thought of resisting. He'd kept receding, and she'd kept moving toward him, no volition involved. Then she had been within touching distance, and nothing had remained in her stalled mind but…wow. *Wow.*

Even at five-foot-ten with four-inch heels, she was dwarfed by him. Besides his towering height, his shoulders, torso and arms were daunting, his waist and hips narrow, his thighs formidable. And his legs went on forever.

And that was what she could see through his slate-gray suit. She couldn't even imagine what his body would look like out of it.

But one thing she saw clearly. His face.

Ruthless planes and stark angles composed his forehead, nose and jaw. His cheekbones slashed so sharply against his polished teak skin, she felt she could cut herself on them. His lips were sculpted from decadent sensuality. Put together, his features were a standard of male beauty no one would ever come close to measuring up to. Not in her eyes.

But what captivated her went beyond his physical endowments and sexual magnetism. It wasn't even those stormy eyes, surrounded by lashes as raven-black as the layers of his vital hair, and slanted to the same mysterious angle as his dense eyebrows. It was the entity that looked back at her through them.

Then he'd thanked her, for coming when he'd *summoned* her.

The dark spell of his voice hadn't stopped annoyance from registering at his arrogance. Even when nothing else could describe the way she'd walked to him as if in thrall. Then he'd cupped her cheek and the world disappeared.

Nothing was left but his touch, and the building urge for something…more. And he gave her more. Like a hungry panther, he backed her against the wall only to hover over her lips, tantalizing her with the dizzying scent of his maleness and desire.

She started trembling, fearing her heart would stop if he didn't kiss her. Then he did. And that intensity between them manifested into a literal spark, zapping what remained of her coherence. She looked up into his eyes when he jerked away, confessing her helplessness. And a change came over him.

As overriding as his approach had been up till that point, there'd been restraint in it. But now his eyes explicitly said there'd be none from this point forward. He wouldn't stop at a kiss. He wanted more. Everything. Then he told her just that.

Yes, my beauty, yes. Everything with me. Now.

On some level, she realized this was insane. But when he swept her up into his arms, she melted in his hold, let him take her wherever he would.

Then he crossed into a semidark room, an opulent study. He set her back on her feet only to press her against the door. Before she could draw another breath, he thrust his tongue deeper in her mouth as he undid her hair clip. Her hair swished down over his hand, and he combed his fingers through it, sending pleasure cascading to every root. Then his other hand found her zipper and slid it down.

She moaned a sound she'd never before produced—the sound of relief-laced shock—as her bodice released her breasts with a rustling sigh. His lips swallowed her moans, drugging her with delight. One thing kept repeating in her brain.

She'd wake up any moment now.

But she didn't wake up. And now she knew she wouldn't.

This was just too overwhelming to be a dream.

This was real.

Another shock zigzagged through her as his fingers splayed against her back, and her flesh almost burst into flame. She jerked away from the burning, then pressed back for more. And he took his onslaught to the next level.

He yanked up her skirt, cupped her buttocks beneath her panties and hauled her up against him. She gasped at his grip over her intimate flesh, at his effortless power. Gasps became moans as he ground the steel of his erection against her core, flooding it with another rush of liquid heat.

Something scalding rumbled from him as he tugged one thigh, splaying her around his hips. Then he thrust against her to the same rhythm his tongue plunged inside her mouth.

His powerful chest rubbed against her breasts, the friction of their remaining clothes pricking her nipples into pin-points of agony.

She trembled in his hold as his lips burned a trail from her lips down to her neck, settling there to ravage her with tugging kisses that sent pleasure hurtling through her blood with each savage pull.

It felt as if all existence converged on him, became him, his body and breath, his hands and mouth. She was no lon-ger herself, but a mass of needs wrapped around him, open to him. The flowing throb between her legs escalated to a pounding that needed *something* to assuage it. When it tipped into sheer discomfort, she cried out.

He shuddered against her, as if her cry electrified him, then he snapped his head up and crashed his lips on her wide-open mouth, thrusting deeply.

She plunged into his taste again as his tongue dueled with hers, as his lips and teeth mastered her. This was nothing like the slow seduction she'd imagined her first intimate encounter would be. This was an invasion, a ravaging. And she wanted it that way.

In unison with her feverish need, he snatched her off her feet again, crossed the room. Lowering her on a massive couch that would accommodate his full length, he straight-ened and looked down at her. In the dim light coming from somewhere in the spacious room, his gaze reflected the il-lumination, sparkled silver, devouring her. Hers druggedly luxuriated in gliding over his awe-striking figure.

Then he finally came down over her, his powerful limbs a prison of muscle and maleness.

"Estou louco de desejo por você, minha beleza única."

I'm mad with wanting you, my unique beauty.

She would have said the same to him, if she could. But all she could do was silently arch up to help him when his hands dipped beneath her to undo her bra. He peeled it off and spilled her swollen breasts into his palms. She lurched as he growled his appreciation, pressing them together, mitigating their ache, heightening her fever. Then he bent and showed her there was more exquisite agony, grazing one nipple then the other with his teeth, swirling them with his hot tongue. By the time he suckled them, she was writhing beneath him as he built to long, hard pulls.

Then he blew his scorching confessions on them. "You made me lose my mind with a look. Then I touched you, tasted you, felt you like this, beneath me, open for me, needing me."

She could only nod jerkily, her teeth starting to clatter as his hands squeezed her buttocks, then slid her soaked panties off her quivering legs. He then discarded his jacket, undid his shirt and flung it open before pressing back over her. His silky hair-roughened flesh rubbed her into a frenzy, then suddenly…he stilled.

Disentangling their bodies, he rose on extended arms and loomed above her. "You're trembling all over. Are you afraid?"

Surprise made words catch in her swollen throat. "O-only that my heart might stop…or I might faint."

Something more dangerous than anything he'd exposed her to spread on his face. A smile. Predatory, starved, unbearably arousing. "I feel the same. Minus the fainting. My heart might stop if I don't have you naked beneath me." But instead of extracting her from her undone dress, he bunched it at her midriff. "Next time, I'll worship you from your lashes to your toenails. But now I need to be inside you. Say you need me, too. Say you can't wait. Say it."

There was no voice left in her. She was coming apart, the pounding in her core rising to a frantic hammering. Her head jerked on a nod, a tear slipping from her left eye.

He swooped down, closed his lips over her earlobe, catching the moisture. With his first nip, she arched up into his arousal with a cry, her legs falling open, giving him license to take, to possess.

His breathing as harsh as hers, he rose to his knees, and in barely suppressed urgency, released himself. Her heart rammed her ribs. With intimidation at the size of him.

Then he took his erection in his hand, and she could only lie there, waiting for him to do whatever it took to satisfy this gnawing hunger. Her heart thundered, expecting him to drive into her, filling that maddening emptiness he'd created inside her, bracing for the pain. But he didn't, only squeezed his eyes shut on what sounded like a vicious curse. When he opened them, they almost vaporized her. Then pushing her thighs wider apart, his hand slid beneath her, tilting her hips. His gaze swept downward, dragging hers with it. With a stuttering heart, she watched him open the engorged lips of her sex, then, making no attempt to penetrate her, he rubbed the scorching length of his manhood between them.

The pleasure was so acute she bowed up on a shrill cry.

His other hand clenched her buttocks, he bent and clamped her lips in a fierce kiss.

"Do you feel how wet and hot and ready for me you are?"

He glided up, nudging her most sensitive knot of flesh. She shrieked in his mouth, ecstasy almost too sharp to bear. He circled her swollen knot with his crown until everything in the world focused on the point where his flesh tormented hers.

"Please, please…"

She pleaded with him even when she didn't know if she could accommodate him. But this…this was what she'd been waiting for all her life. This was why she'd never been tempted to share her body with a man. Because she'd never experienced anything like this mind-searing, caution-annihilating lust.

His lips possessed hers again, swallowing her pleas as he thrust against her, prodding her nub over and over.

The pleasure became an unbearable pressure that clamored to unfurl. When she felt she could stand it no more, he quickened his tempo and snapped the tension inside her.

He pinned her beneath him as she bucked and shrieked, release tearing through her. Continuing to pump his hardness against her quivering flesh, he drained her of the last spasm of pleasure her body needed to discharge.

She slumped beneath him, depleted, sated, her intoxicated gaze fixed on him as he rose to his knees between her splayed legs. Pumping his erection, groans gusted from his depths as he climaxed, his blazing eyes never leaving hers.

She'd never known anything as incredible as the sight and sound of him in the grip of orgasm, nor felt anything as fulfilling as knowing she'd given him as much pleasure as he'd given her. Breathing slowing down, she spiraled into a chasm of satisfaction and melted deeper into the plushness beneath her....

Awareness flooded back into her as she felt him gently wiping her belly before he came down over her, claiming her lips in luxurious kisses. It was as if after devouring her, he was now sipping her, savoring her. Each clinging kiss solidified the intimacy they'd shared, and told her the explosive episode had been a prelude to a deeper passion.

When he finally raised his head it was to reach above her. A light burst on. Even though it was soft and soothing, her eyes squeezed shut. When she opened them again, she found him looking down at her indulgently.

"What—what just happened?"

She hadn't intended to speak. Certainly not to say something that moronic. But she had, her voice deep, husky and nothing like she'd ever heard it.

Expecting ridicule to enter his gaze, his hypnotic eyes only turned serious. "No idea. Nothing like this has ever happened to me before. But if I have to guess, I'd say... magic."

Relief swamped her. He didn't consider her bewilderment an act, or stupid. And he felt the same way.

She exhaled in relief. "In the absence of any other explanation, I'd have to agree."

Yet now with the madness-inducing arousal sated, embarrassment started to submerge her.

What had she done?

She sank deeper into what she now saw was an oversize, dark green and gold silk brocade couch, acutely conscious of their state of undress, of every inch of his flesh that was still pressed into her most intimate parts.

As if attuned to her needs, as he'd seemed to be from the start, he rose off her, slid to the ground and kneeled beside her. After forcing his unabated erection into his pants, he retrieved her panties. Navigating the high-heeled shoes he'd left on her, he slid the panties over her shaking legs, caressing and kissing his way from her foot up. Her senses had ignited all over again as he fitted the damp garment back on her hips. And that was before he pressed a hot kiss on her core through the fabric, and almost blew out any fuse left intact in her brain.

As she struggled to deal with the new blow, he rearranged her skirt over her legs, then eased her up to a sitting position. He was so tall he was on her same level even on his knees. Before he pulled her bodice up, he cupped her heavy breasts in his large palms and saluted each gloriously sore nipple with a soft kiss. Every string holding her up gave. She slumped forward against his endless chest.

He received her weight with a shuddering groan. Then after a final kneading caress, he scooped her breasts back in her bra, rearranged the bodice over them, reached behind her and pulled her zipper up.

Brushing her hair back, he cupped her jaw and claimed her parted lips. He drew back, pausing for a moment before he came back over her, plundering her lips and body.

Deepening their kiss, he rose and pushed her back against the couch. When he finally tore his lips away, her head was swimming and her body had ignited all over again.

"It's actually physically painful to stop ravishing you." His teeth gritted. "I thought taking the edge off would cool us down long enough for us to get introduced. Seems I was wrong."

"Ellie." Her name left her in a rush as he moved to gather her to him again. Her heart would burst if he resumed kissing her. "My name is Ellie."

"Ellie." He frowned as he sat back, repeated the name as if tasting it. Then he shook his head. "It doesn't suit you."

"Why, thanks!"

His lips pursed at her sarcasm, an imperious eyebrow raised in disapproval. "How could your parents see the glorious baby you must have been and give you such a nondescript name? Ellie? What's that supposed to mean?"

"My parents actually gave me a pretty lofty name. I extracted a nickname from it as everyone thinks it makes me sound like a character from a medieval play."

"I take back my condemnation of your parents if they gave you a distinguished name. What is it?"

"Eliana."

His eyes suddenly grew soft. "Eliana. God has answered."

He understood the meaning of her name. He was the first one to ever do so.

He took her hand, pressed his lips in her palm. "Now, *that* is you. You must have been their every prayer answered. As you are the answer to my every fantasy."

Her blood blazed as it rushed to her cheeks. "You're poetic, too? Isn't it enough you're…all that?" She made an encompassing gesture, then rushed to splay a hand over his chest as he surged toward her. "We aren't anywhere near introduced yet, and if you touch and kiss me again I—I…"

"You'll catch fire again."

She turned her head against the couch. "I can't deal with the way I did the first time, so give me a chance to..."

A gentle finger on her chin brought her eyes back to his. "I thought I was imagining it before, but you *are* shy."

"Pretty laughable, I know, after...after..."

"You went up in flames in my arms?" he completed for her again. "I find your shyness no such thing. But I felt it even through your mind-blowing response." She hid her face in his chest, felt his chuckle rev below her cheek. "Don't be even shier now. You affected me the same way, minus the shyness part. *Meu Deus*...the way you surrendered to me, as if you couldn't help yourself, as if I'd overwhelmed you."

"No 'as if' about it. You more than overwhelmed me." She burrowed deeper into him, arousal mingling with relief as he crushed her harder in his embrace.

So this was what desire was all about. This was what had been missing all her life. Him. She must have felt him out there, have instinctively known that accepting anything less, with anyone else, would be shortchanging herself.

Out loud, she whispered, "So this is the kind of crazy attraction that drives people to commit insanities, huh?"

His beautiful lips curved. "Delightful insanities."

She couldn't have put it better. "Yes."

"But even in my insanity, some fail-safe mechanism kicked in and pulled me back from possessing you without protection."

She gaped at him. That hadn't even crossed her mind!

Then the enormity of the whole situation hit her. Hard.

He smoothed a hand over her flaming cheek. "I only did so for you. Another unprecedented thing for me."

"You mean you usually don't consider your...partner?" she croaked, reeling with belated shock at her own folly.

"I usually consider my partner *and* myself. This time I only considered you. This was so out of the blue, progressed with such blinding speed...at the last moment I thought you might not even realize what you were risking. So even though it was beyond me to stop pleasuring you, I had to protect you."

"Oh…" She found no words to express what she was feeling. This was…huge. He could have just taken his pleasure, but he hadn't. He'd put her safety before his own carnal needs. Her hands squeezed his arm in gratitude, loving the sheer power her fingers felt beneath them. "Thank you."

He gathered her tighter to him and planted a kiss on her forehead. "Anything for you, *minha beleza,* anything at all." He drew away to look down at her. "But now that I'm not about to have a heart attack with arousal, I will procure all precautions, and props."

Props? The word ricocheted in her imagination as he leveled the full force of his gaze on her.

"Give me your promise."

"Wh-what promise?"

"That you'll spend the night in my arms."

"Oh…"

She *really* had to stop saying that!

"Then after this night, the next night. And the next."

Throat closing at his intensity, she murmured, "Wouldn't you want to see how one night goes before committing to more?"

"I know how this night will go. I will pleasure you to within an inch of your life, make it impossible for you not to crave more." At her head shake his eyebrow rose again, what she felt certain sent powerful men cowering. "How can you think this won't happen?"

"Because I have no idea if *I* can make it impossible for *you* not to crave more nights."

"Have I blown a fuse in there with too much pleasure already?" One finger gently tapped her temple, his smile lazy assurance itself. "It's the only explanation as to why you'd even consider something so ludicrous."

"If you say so," she mumbled.

"I do. Now give me your promise." At her hesitation, he frowned. "Are you worried I might turn out to be a nutcase?"

She coughed. "That is one thing that didn't even cross my mind."

"So you're saying you trust me?" He dragged his teeth along her neck like a vampire searching for the sweetest spot for a bite. Her head fell back, giving him the exposure he needed to find the best one.

A shudder of acute pleasure shook her whole frame as he took that nip. "I'm saying I couldn't even think about anything beyond what you made me feel. If you didn't notice, I haven't exactly been functioning on any logical level since you…'summoned me.'"

He raised his head, pure male satisfaction gleaming in his eyes. "No, you haven't. But neither have I."

It was so gratifying that he confessed her equal effect on him so openly. "I was and still am operating purely on instinct."

"And your instincts are telling you to trust me?"

"I can't explain it—" she dived into him again, nodding against his hot-velvet flesh "—but they do." She looked up, whispering what felt like a pledge. "I do trust you."

His eyes blazed in response. "Implicitly?"

She nodded again.

"You won't freak out when I make unusual demands in bed?"

Her eyes grew wider as his filled with that predator's gleam that made her pulse race in anticipation.

Still, she had to ask. "Define unusual."

"Unusual in quantity…not quality." Before she could tell him that wasn't much better, he added, "At least, not too unusual in quality."

"There you go again with unrealistic expectations."

His lips twisted. "You think I'm false advertising?"

"It's me who has performance…or rather conformance anxiety. I don't think I can meet your demands in quantity. It's out of the question I could in quality."

"Just leave everything to me. As you've done so far." He took her on his lap, caressing her all over. "Any complaints?"

"Only one." She fidgeted over the massive hardness beneath her, the simmering inside her flaring up again. "That you seem to have created a monster."

Those perfect teeth flashed as he pressed her against his arousal. "You want more."

"I want *you*," she moaned.

"Not as much as I want you. Ah-ah-ah…" He placed a silencing finger on her lips when she started to protest. "You just have to trust me again on this. Now…your promise."

She pushed out of his arms, trying to scramble off his lap. "I can't. My brain feels like I was in a collision and I…"

He let her separate them, his face suddenly chiseled from granite. "Are you regretting it?"

"God, *no*. It was…beyond magical. But…but…"

"It's too much, too fast."

She nodded, anxiously probing his reaction. And it felt as if a cool balm had spread over her burning flesh. There was only self-deprecation on his lips, empathy in his eyes.

After the way she'd surrendered to him, another man would have accused her of leading him on, then playing hard to get. A few men had even called her a tease.

But he wasn't like those men. He was like no other.

She wanted to kiss him for being so wonderful. But a kiss might destroy his control, the only thing that stopped *her* from getting in over her head. More than she already had, that was.

"It isn't too much or too fast, not for me," he said, his voice a dark caress. "Every second with you is how I'll define perfection from now on. But I will slow down—for you." He swept her into his arms again and she succumbed on a ragged sigh, sank back into the luxury of his embrace. "But there are so many more intimacies I need to share with you, many untold pleasures. I need to keep kissing and touching and talking to you. So when everyone goes away, you'll stay."

"Yes." Then she frowned. "But what do you mean *stay?*"

"The night. In my bed. In my arms."

"I got that. But stay where?"

"Stay here, of course."

"*You're* staying here?"

"I should think so. I own the place."

And suddenly, all the details she'd missed—in him, in what he'd said, which should have made sense before now but hadn't—coalesced. Into one big wrecking ball.

It swung into her so hard, it knocked her out of his arms again. "You're...*him?*"

Three

Ellie gaped at the man who'd given her her life's most intense experience. He was…he was…

"I've been referred to in some extremely unflattering ways before," he drawled. "'Him' wasn't among them."

"I mean *you're*…that man?"

"'That man' is also not what I want to hear on your lips."

"God…it's just… Okay, stop! Let me breathe." Shaking her head, she splayed her hand on his chest as if to ward him off, but really to steady herself. "You're…Moreno Salazar?"

He took her fluttering hand to his lips. "To you…I am only Rafael." He punctuated his words by suckling each finger. "You will moan my name into my lips…scream it against my flesh…all through the night."

She was a molten mass by the time he pulled her other hand, wound her arms around his neck. But she still had to say…something. Anything.

"But you said you won't make love to me."

That wasn't the issue here. Or what she'd meant to say.

He kissed the arms hanging limply around his neck. "I think I proved there are other ways of pleasuring you."

"But I thought you understood, agreed that I need to— to…"

"Regroup? Yes, I know. And I won't do anything to cross your comfort zone anymore."

This man seemed to be reading her hectic mind, defusing her agitation, saying just the right thing.

But… "That's still not it."

"Then what is it?"

"You even have to ask? It's who you are. It changes everything."

His lips stilled on the sensitive flesh of her inner arm, then he raised his head, a spectacular frown descending over his leonine brow. "It changes nothing. I'm still the man you lost your mind over, the man you wanted with every fiber of your being. And that's the man I'll remain to you."

"Yes, but you're also Rafael Moreno Salazar, and I'm here attending your ball because my…boss is here to court your favor. And this complicates everything."

"This complicates nothing, I tell you."

"Oh, but it does. It tangles business with pleasure in a way I couldn't have expected in my wildest dreams. Now I can't spend the night with you. I don't even know how everything will be affected by what we've already shared."

Ellie's arms slid off his shoulders and she slumped back. She felt as if he'd hurtled out of her reach when just minutes ago she'd felt he was closer to her than anyone had ever been.

She pitched forward, dropped her head in trembling hands. "Oh, God, why couldn't you have just turned out to be just another guest here, just a regular man?"

"Well, I'm not." He pulled her back into the cradle of his arm. "Which is why I can have you. A regular man wouldn't dream of coming near you." Before she could scoff at the exaggeration he'd said with such conviction, he went on just as seriously, "But I don't care that business interests are involved. I'm even thankful they are, since they brought you here. I'm in your boss's eternal debt for being the reason I met you. So if he is any good, I'll do business with him. And that will have nothing to do with us."

She squirmed to put some distance between them. "How can you say that in the same breath you say you'd do business with my boss for me?"

"I did stipulate he be at least 'any good' at what he does. I won't prove my interest in you by gambling on a losing proposition. I'm into winning and would go to any constructive lengths to win you."

"Constructive lengths." A giggle escaped her. "Now, that's an innovative way of putting it. Though you didn't have to go to any lengths, constructive or otherwise. You stood there and cast your spell, and I ran and flung myself into your arms."

"You neither ran nor flung yourself. But you will."

She sighed, acknowledging his confidence. "So will you always be the magnet, with me the helpless iron filings, or is there hope of you doing some running yourself?"

"Command me, and I'll run as long and as hard as you wish." His fervor felt so real. But why not, when she felt the same? "I *would* have run to you this time, too, but I had to draw you away from the crowd."

Something slotted in her mind with a thud. "You didn't intend to make an appearance tonight, did you?"

His shrug was dismissive. "Whatever my intentions, I saw you…and nothing else mattered after that."

"Same here. But you were going to pull another no-show tonight, right? Do you keep gathering people so you can watch them when they think you're not around? Is this your method of vetting prospective partners?"

"It's currently a partner. In the singular."

"Oh. I didn't realize you're looking for only one."

"I am." The flare in his eyes said he was no longer talking about a *business* partner.

A thrill darted through her, and she sighed as he gathered her closer, soaking up his warmth and desire. "You do know the moment you touch me you nullify my thought processes, don't you?"

"Not touching you is like holding my breath. I can only do it for so many minutes at a time. So will you stop pulling away? We can discuss whatever you like, for as long as you like, just with you in my arms."

Sighing again, she relaxed in his hold, resigned to the fact that she wasn't strong enough to resist both her need and his.

His lips curved. "So you think I'd judge those I'm considering for such a vital partnership by spying on them in a party? Would I disqualify them for stepping on their partner's feet or talking with their mouth full?"

"I bet you'd see everything you need to make an accurate judgment in observations like those. Just like you always do."

His eyebrows rose. "How do you know what I always do?"

"Are you kidding? The past couple of hours are worth a year of intensive…exposure. And I'm connecting what I've just learned about you with what I've long known of you."

"And what, pray tell, do you think you know about me?"

"Well, as a virtuoso in your field, you have such nonlinear, multidimensional analytic powers, you have the world begging for your Midas touch. You got where you are by judging every situation and person you've dealt with throughout your career perfectly. As perfectly as you judged me from a literal hundred paces."

He wove his fingers into her hair, wrapped a handful around his wrist and inhaled it. "Get yourself out of any comparison. Nothing with you had anything to do with anything I've ever experienced before. There was no judgment involved on my part, not when you zapped me from a literal hundred paces, too. And you did that to me when I had my back to you."

She blinked. "Really?"

"Really. I was at the mezzanine when your aura lashed me with a thousand volts of delight." He bent and kissed the tops of her breasts that bulged above the now too-tight bodice. "We've already agreed there was magic at work."

"Yes." There was no contradicting him on that point. "So you're not orchestrating events only to watch the attendees, at least to weed out those who prove to be blatantly unsuitable?"

"Don't you think someone as exceptional as you advertise me to be would let résumés choose for me?"

Suddenly she realized what was going on. They'd moved from blinding passion, bypassing any expected awkwardness in the wake of its temporary sating, and plunged right into delightful banter. The seamlessness of it all had her heart soaring.

She cupped his jaw, luxuriating in the ruggedness that filled her palm. "I would have thought so, if you haven't just promised to give my boss preferential treatment if he passes the lamentable level of 'any good.' Or maybe I just mess with your thought processes, too."

Blistering intensity suddenly filled his eyes, making her heart falter. Then he covered her hand with his. "Do you realize this is the first time you've touched me?"

Her mouth dropped open. "I've been touching you non-stop since about a minute and a half after setting eyes on you."

"No. You didn't touch me once. You let me touch you. This is your first voluntary touch."

She gaped at him, everything rewinding and replaying. And he was right. She hadn't touched him once!

She'd just stood or lain there and let him do whatever he wanted, inciting him only by total surrender.

"I was too overwhelmed to do anything but let you possess me. But let me compensate both of us."

Her other hand reached for his face, gliding up his cheek, moaning at the wonder of his feel, before doing what she'd been aching to do. She slipped her fingers into the hair at his nape, and the thick mass slid like living silk between them, urging her to take more. His breath caught as she bunched a handful of his locks, then tugged.

Next second she was flat on her back, with him on top of her, hips driving between her spread thighs, his febrile, wrenching kisses no longer resembling his previous ones.

Her reaction was an even fuller submission. And a deeper madness. Now that she was aware of the risks, she wanted to release him from his promise, tell him to just take her now, come what may.

But to her dismay, Rafael only tore his lips from hers. Flinging himself off her, he sat up and pitched forward, both forearms resting on his knees, hair raining over his forehead to hide his eyes as he struggled to regulate his harsh breathing.

"I thought touching you was mind-altering…but you touching me is insanity inducing." He slanted her a voracious glance as he took her hands and pulled her up. "Leave the touching to me tonight. Until I train myself to withstand your touch without pouncing on you and ravishing you."

Trembling all over, she sat up, every cell in her body rioting against his decree. She now wanted nothing but to touch him, craved nothing but his ravishing. Even thinking of the consequences wasn't deterring her. Which did prove that exposure to him *was* insanity inducing.

But it meant so much, that he'd applied brakes—for her—against the demands of his very…obvious desires. It meant even more that he confessed to a weakness. Something Rafael Moreno Salazar had never exhibited in the eight years of his meteoric rise to the top of a field he'd singlehandedly revolutionized.

The fact that *that* man and *her* man were one and the same was still too much to get her head around. She hadn't even started to scratch the surface of the implications. No matter what he said, she knew being who he was *would* cause problems.

But for now she had him, in those moments of perfection when she was the world to him. As he was to her. And really, what was the point of looking ahead? She had no illusions there would be a continuation once they exited this magical interlude.

But they were still there now.

Feeling she'd be poking a dragon, yet unable to stop, she slid her hand across his shoulders, caressing her way down his back to his waist, delving beneath his open shirt and repeating the journey up, then down, then lower still. The exquisite pleasure of having this freedom, this privilege, was intoxicating.

He caught her against him, crushing her in his arms, his face set in stark lines of savage hunger. And she did another first. She brought his lips down to hers.

Initiating this kiss made it so different, enabling her to set its taste and temperature, sweet and scalding at once. He let her savor him—for about thirty seconds. Then he pushed out of her arms, exploded to his feet.

He scowled down at her. "If you don't want to be on your back, naked and with me buried all the way inside you, you better not touch or kiss me again."

She rubbed the heel of her hand against the itch behind her breastbone. "And you better find a shortcut in your training because now that I've touched and kissed you, I don't want to do anything else."

"You better stop saying things like that, too. They have the same effect on me."

Her lids grew heavier as she slumped under the weight of craving. "Whatever you say."

He took an explosive step toward her, before stopping, vibrating with control. Then he gritted, "Enchantress."

She sighed, rubbing the itch harder. "Sorcerer."

Suddenly his lips spread into a wide smile as he sat down, keeping a two-inch no-touching zone between them.

"I'm keeping score of your transgressions, and I'll get satisfaction for each and every one. But first, I need the subject of business closed permanently." Seriousness suddenly replaced his intimate teasing. "It won't be preferential when I give your boss precedence over equally qualified candidates. Personal preference *is* an acceptable decisive factor when all things are equal. He might not land *the* partnership, but for you, I'll give him something he's worthy of. I bet he's way above 'any good.' You wouldn't work for someone inept."

Giving in to wild impulse, she combed the raven satin away from his forehead, her breath catching as his eyes flared and his whole body tensed. "On what do you base such belief?" Suddenly a suspicion hit her. "You don't think I rely on something other than my professional skills, do you?"

The darkening of pained arousal in his eyes abruptly became affront. "What? *No*. That's something I'd feel at a *thousand* paces." He took her by the shoulders, his face set in adamant lines. "A major part of the judgment you so laud is instinct, and that told me everything I need to know about you. And then, your effect on me transcends my judgment, not nullifies it. Now that I choose to employ it, I can see you're acutely intelligent but burdened with unwavering integrity. You'd only rely on your personal merits no matter how many more lucrative paths were at your disposal."

Her eyes glazed over his lips. Everything he said was so lyrical, it kept deepening his spell. And beyond that, and his hypnotic voice, there was that accent she couldn't pinpoint. And it was the sexiest thing she'd ever heard.

And if that wasn't enough, and he'd ignite her while reciting the ingredients of a salad dressing bottle, he'd gone and said all those incredible things about her. No one had ever held her in such high regard before. And for it to come from Rafael Moreno Salazar—a man whose analyses governments and giant multinational corporations paid millions for—that was beyond enormous.

She surged, clung to his lips in a kiss of gratitude.

By the time she swooned away and lay back, transported by his taste and testimony, he was growling like a starving lion.

"You're treading nonexistent ice, Eliana."

Hearing the name she'd never liked on *his* lips, enunciated with such elegance and command, she suddenly loved it. In fact, she couldn't imagine him calling her anything else.

She sat up, pressed another kiss to his jaw. "You can't say things like that and expect me not to pounce on you."

Unlocking his gritted teeth, he shot her a warning glance. "I'd stake my history as an unerring analyst on every word's accuracy. And if your agency warranted an invite…" He raised an eyebrow. "I assume your boss *is* invited?"

She giggled. "I assure you he's not gate-crashing."

"Then this validates my theory that he is way above the 'any good' level. And if he invited you, then you have a prominent position within his agency. And to have that so young, you must be superlative in your specialty."

"I'm not *that* young."

"I know you're over eighteen. If not by much. I'm almost having dirty old man pangs here."

"You're only thirty-two!"

His lips twisted at her exclamation. "You've researched

me well. But that still makes me ten or more years older than you are. You can't be more than twenty-one."

"I'll be twenty-four in three months."

His eyebrows rose, but he only said, "That's less than three years older than my estimate."

"Three years make a huge difference. Especially to me. I graduated high school two years early, earned my undergraduate degree almost four years ago and I'm on my second masters degree now. And because of my home environment, I've had hands-on experience in my current job since I was twelve."

"See? My analysis was accurate. You follow no rules, and your prowess has nothing to do with your age." He tugged her flush against him, spoke against her lips, singeing her with his breath and words. "And I've changed my mind. Forget your boss. I'll steal you away from him. Name your terms. Whatever they are, I'll meet them."

That made her push him away. "Stop right there. For God's sake, you don't even know what my specialty is!"

His shrug was self-assurance incarnate as he stretched her back on the couch and came down full-length beside her. "Whatever it is, I always need unique minds and exceptional talents on my team. It's how my conglomerate got so big so fast, by offering candidates everything they'd never get anywhere else in terms of freedom, resources and remuneration."

She did know that. But never in a million years had she imagined she'd be headhunted by him under any circumstances. And for him to do that while they lay entwined like this…

She feebly pushed at him as he bent to nuzzle her neck. "I do know your methods, but…no, okay? This wouldn't only complicate matters…it would mess them up beyond repair. People still think I got my current position because of nepotism. With you, they'd think I got it because…"

"Because you send me out of my mind with desire and it's literally painful to keep my hands off you?" He gathered her tighter against him. "I can't describe how profoundly indifferent I am to what people think. You're exactly the kind of rare talent I aggressively pursue."

"*Rare…?* Come on!"

"You said I got where I am by reading people perfectly. I read you better than I've ever read anyone. So you either don't know how rare you are or are too modest or too held back by other's opinions. I'm the one to free you from all that, the one to give you everything you need to fulfill your potential. You are exactly what I need. On all fronts."

She stared into his eyes, head spinning. He had no reason to sweet-talk her. She'd already promised him the night. And as many nights as he'd want her. He meant all that.

A smile broke his intensity. "But as I'll take it slow in courting you in pleasure, I will do the same as I court you in business."

"Don't. Please, Rafael…"

He shuddered against her, his fingers digging into her buttocks, grinding her into his hardness. "Yes, say my name. Say it, *minha beleza.*"

"*Rafael.*" That came out a long moan of protest. "Please… stop talking about business in any form. I want to keep things purely like this—between us, man to woman. This is all that matters to me."

He eased his hold on her, rose on his elbow, brooding down at her. Then he exhaled. "As you wish. For now."

Then in one impossible move, he was on his feet with her swept up in his powerful embrace. She wrapped her arms around his neck, not to secure herself or to help him, but because she loved it.

He smiled down at her. "You must be starving. Let's dine while we wait the ball out, and then…"

She jackknifed, making him spill her to her feet.

"I have to get back to the ball!"

He detained her as she whirled away. "You certainly do not. You didn't want to be there in the first place."

As her gaze darted around, searching for her purse, his words sank in. "How do you know I didn't want to come?"

His smile was all knowing, as she was really beginning to think he was. "I told you I can read you."

Something hot and sweet expanded inside her. He did interpret her so accurately it was scary. Wonderfully so.

She caressed his hard cheek and he caught her hand, buried his lips in her palm. "I'll never stop being thankful that I dragged myself here. But I do have to go find my...boss. He must think I've driven off a cliff by now."

After a moment's contemplation, he let go of her hand and walked away. He located the purse that had fallen from her what felt like days ago by the door.

He brought it back to her. "Call your boss. Give him some excuse for not attending the ball."

Ellie blinked up at him. "Now that you mention calling, I can't imagine how he hasn't called me a million times." She pounced on her purse...and groaned when she didn't find her phone. "I must have left my phone in the car, or even back in the apartment. I was half-asleep at the time. Oh, God, he must be going out of his mind thinking something happened to me."

Rafael frowned, but silently bent to reach for his jacket. Producing his phone, he handed it to her.

She shook her head. "I'd have to explain why I'm calling from someone else's phone, whose it is—and I assume you don't want me to tell him it's yours?"

"I don't mind."

She rolled her eyes. "I do. You have no idea the interrogation your name would instigate. And I don't want to invent a story. I'll just go reassure him in person."

She turned away and he buttoned up his shirt, tucked it

in, shrugged on his jacket and fell in step with her, taking her around the waist. "I'm not letting you out of my sight."

She kissed his chest. "I'll only be ten minutes."

"Not one minute. Not without me."

She leaned her head against his shoulder, loving his unyielding…everything. There was no point in arguing. This man got what he wanted. Period. And she was what he wanted now. Who was she to stand in the way of his desires?

Sighing her pleasure, she still had to point out the obvious. "Though I never found photos of you, I can't say I looked very hard. What if someone out there did and recognizes you? Your plan to keep stirring the marketing scene into butter with your elusiveness will come to an abrupt end."

"I'll be worth not letting you out of my sight."

Delight heightening, she teased, "But if people recognize you, you'll be swamped. This might postpone our…plans."

"If I suspect it will, I'll go on a rampage and chase everybody out." He pressed an openmouthed kiss on her lips. "Now quit stalling."

Laughing, tucked into his side, she walked out of the study where her life had changed forever, feeling she was stepping out into a new universe filled with endless possibility. A universe with him at its center.

For however long she had with him.

Walking back to the ballroom with Eliana, Rafael realized how far away his study was. When he'd been carrying her there, it had only felt ten paces away.

"This place is amazing."

He looked down at the magnificent human flower nestled into his side. He felt as if her flesh was an extension of his, her smile and voice and eyes the fuel of his heartbeats. The past hours had been the most incredible, ecstatic stretch of life he'd ever had.

She was looking around as she strode by his side, as if it was the first time she'd seen the place. It was. She'd had eyes only for him on her first passage through it.

He nuzzled her cheek, truly unable to stop touching her. "It was a mansion that was converted into a boutique hotel. I was driving down the coast when I saw it and decided to spend the night. The next day, I bought it. I refurbished it but preserved most of what I liked about it in the first place."

Her eyes poured that all-out appreciation over him, not attempting to temper it or to hide how much she loved being with him. "It must have tremendous tourist appeal, especially in its current lavish condition."

"I didn't buy it for commercial purposes."

Her eyes widened. "You plan to live here?"

In the space of a heartbeat, he saw a whole lifetime in which he did—with her. But something stopped him from sharing the vision when so far he'd been telling her everything as it occurred to him. Probably out of fear he'd alarm her, as he had when he'd made those business offers. It had been only then that she'd resisted him. He wouldn't risk another premature move.

"I haven't thought about it." He'd only had revenge on his mind since he'd come to Brazil. Until he'd seen her. Now anything but her felt inconsequential. "I always acquire whatever my gut tells me to, then decide what to do with my acquisitions later. This place presented the best setting for this ball. But though I'm used to living in spacious, isolated places, this mansion might be too much for only me."

"You have no one to share the place with…?" She stopped, mortification suddenly flooding her gaze, stiffening her body. "It didn't even occur to me to ask if you have a—a family."

Thanks to Ferreira, he no longer did.

But that wasn't the family she was asking about. She

was belatedly horrified at almost sleeping with a man who might turn out to be married.

Before entering the ballroom, he took her by the shoulders. "Do I transmit sleazy cheater vibes to you?"

That delightful flush flamed across her cheekbones as her eyes escaped his rebuking ones. "You know what vibes you transmit to me. The kind that short-circuit my mind."

He raised her face to his, felt a pang at the uncertain vulnerability in her eyes. Hugging her fiercely, he knew he'd do anything to never see that look in her eyes again.

"Even short-circuiting, you pegged me right in every way. I have no one, *minha beleza*. I'm totally free to worship you. As I will. From now on."

Her eyes cleared at once. And she didn't question his "from now on" statement the way she had when he'd proposed nightly meetings before. He was grateful because he no longer considered those enough. He now realized what it meant to want someone constantly in his life. It was how he wanted her.

He realized something else: What he saw in those enchanting eyes shouldn't be there, according to logic and the too-limited time they'd had together. But it had been there from the start, was now a blaze that fired his blood, eradicated the cold in the recesses of his heart. Trust. Not limited to her belief in her safety with him, and not the kind he'd seen in his brothers' eyes. This was unique. All hers. And all-out. In him.

Unable to wait to tell her how proud he felt to have it, he took her into the ballroom so they'd conclude this business with her boss and he could have her all to himself again.

A few feet in, it was as if he'd hit a force field head on. And...of course...what but that living storm he had for a partner would cause such a disruption?

Richard was striding toward them. He couldn't wait to brag how right he'd been about Eliana. Not that he expected anything but castigation and scorn. With his brothers seemingly heartless, just like he'd thought he was before finding Eliana, Richard was the one who was truly merciless. As his friend zoomed closer, Rafael saw he wasn't attempting to hide the demon believed to share his body. Not wanting Eliana to see him the first time with it manifested, he shot Richard a warning glance before turning to Eliana with a smile.

"Eliana, please meet my partner, Richard Graves."

Temporarily distracted from searching for her boss, she graciously extended her hand toward Richard. "Pleased to meet you, Mr. Graves."

Richard didn't take her hand, didn't even look at her as he stepped toward Rafael and hissed, "I need a word—*now*."

"Oh, please, go." Eliana spooled away from him, flashing him an exquisite smile even when it was clear Richard's incivility had rattled her. "I'll go finish my own mission."

Before he could stop her or tell Richard what he could do with his word, an erratic movement caught his eye. Ferreira. He was on a collision course with them.

Before any of them could move, Ferreira was pulling Eliana into his arms.

Aggression erupted, almost burst Rafael's head.

He was her boss. And he was on hugging terms with her?

Then the words Ferreira kept saying as he clutched Eliana sank into his mind. Then exploded like depth charges.

"Ellie, a minha menina, você está bem."

Ellie, my baby girl, you're okay.

Rafael stared at the woman he'd lost his mind over, in the arms of the man he was here to destroy.

And everything crashed in place.

Eliana was Ferreira's daughter.

Four

Ellie wished it were true the ground split and swallowed people up. She could have used a vanishing act right now.

First, Rafael's partner ignored her—after a split-second glance that had made her feel that if he ever got her alone, no one would ever find her again.

Then, just as she was trying to pretend to Rafael that his partner's barely leashed aggression hadn't knocked the breath out of her, her father pounced on her out of nowhere.

He was now squeezing her breath out. And swamping her in "baby girls," something they'd agreed he'd never call her in public.

She'd taken the job with his agency over other positions only when he'd promised he'd never give her preferential treatment. But lately she'd been feeling she'd soon be forced to leave, even if she loved her job and was perfect for it. The moment they discovered her boss was her father, no one took her seriously. It was why she hadn't told Rafael. She'd feared he'd reach the same conclusion everyone invariably did. She'd thought this particular bit of info could wait until he got to know her better.

Too late now. She'd been outed in the most embarrassing way. That taught her to get major stuff out of the way first. Not that she considered *that* major. Nothing about her was. It was Rafael who had the market cornered on humongous stuff.

Needing to see his reaction, she struggled to turn her head, but she was inescapably mashed into her father's shoulder. All she could see in her compromised position was Richard Graves. He was striding out of the ballroom, without having that "word" he'd almost dragged Rafael away to have.

At least that reduced the awkwardness. He was one scary dude. She wouldn't wish to meet him in a dark alley, with fewer than the three hundred people around. And Rafael at her side.

Then another thought hit her, pushing her dismay to the maximum.

What could Rafael possibly be thinking about what was happening right now?

"Daddy, oxygen alert."

Her father lurched away at her choking protest, still holding her by the shoulders, his feverish eyes roving over her.

"Where have you been? I drove back to your apartment when I kept getting your voice mail, hoping you'd just fallen asleep. I went out of my mind with worry, banging on the door, knowing how lightly you sleep, thinking you'd fallen and injured yourself…until I remembered you gave me a key. I rushed in to find the place empty and your phone dead and hurried back here hoping you arrived but…"

"I'm *so* sorry you got so worried." She raised her voice over the cacophony of the ball and his frantic reproach, feeling terrible. He'd done over four hours worth of driving. The whole time she'd been with Rafael. "I just got…uh…lost…"

Which was sort of true. She had for a while on the way, initially. Then she had, totally, in Rafael's arms.

Before her father launched into another tirade, she turned him toward Rafael, who was looking at him as if he was some revolting life-form. Probably because he didn't realize who he was. Or found his over-the-top agitation off-putting. Or both.

Wincing at the whole mess, she touched Rafael's arm, feeling a pang at how absolutely vital he'd become to her, how even this simple touch, in this situation, sent her heart scattering its beats at his feet.

"Rafael, this is my father, Teobaldo Ferreira."

Rafael's gaze panned to her and her heart clapped so hard her breath snagged in her throat. There was something in his eyes, something…weird. As if he'd forgotten who she was. Which she had to be imagining. This must be how he looked as his formidable mind processed new situations and variables.

Seeming to gather his wits at last, and even clearly un-sure who Rafael was, or unable to believe he was the same man he was desperate to do business with, her father ex-tended his hand to him.

Rafael stared down at her father's hand.

She winced. She knew he hadn't wanted to make any contact with his candidates tonight, and her father *was* one. But right now, this wasn't about business, but about a simple salute between her overprotective father, and Rafael—the man who'd just demolished the foundations of her existence.

She rose on tiptoe so her words were for his ears only. "Just say hi and leave. I'll catch up with you."

She tried to capture his gaze, to exchange the delight of anticipation of the night to come. Her heart fluttered at the heavy-lidded look in his eyes then stumbled in confusion, as without a word or another look, ignoring her father's hand as his partner had ignored hers, he turned and walked away.

"What was this all about? Who's that man?"

Tearing her stunned gaze away from Rafael's receding back, she looked dazedly at her father, her mind racing.

She didn't want to validate his suspicion about Rafael's identity. If her father realized she was suddenly on such personal terms with the man whose favor he was so fervently hoping to court, he'd subject her to endless interrogation, or ask to be introduced properly—or both. This didn't only mean lost time, but more important a premature crop of those complications she'd predicted. And she didn't want the real world to intervene now, didn't want them to stop being the man and woman who'd found this pure passion for each other, and become the tycoon and the daughter of a hopeful business partner.

But…how could Rafael just leave like that? If he chose not to shake her father's hand because he didn't want any contact with business people tonight, she could understand. It was a bit excessive, stung a little, but she would never bring any issues with her father between them. But the way he'd looked at her, then walked away, even after she'd explained her father's identity…

Stop. Her mind must be playing tricks on her after all the upheavals of the past hours. She must be beyond exhausted now, operating on pure adrenaline…and other hormones. And those weren't conducive to rational observations.

Someone must have caught his eye, someone important he couldn't postpone greeting. Then he'd be back.

"What's going on with you tonight? Talk to me, *querida*."

Blinking, she realized she'd been staring at her father vacantly as her mind churned.

Forcing herself out of her fugue, she gave him a hug, his beloved presence grounding her as it always did. "I'm really so sorry I caused you such worry." Heat rushed to her face with memories of why she had. "I came as soon as I could to reassure you I'm fine. But I have to go now."

"You called that man Rafael. Is he who I think he is?"

Her hungry gaze sought out Rafael, found him standing at the entrance of the ballroom. So he wasn't coming back. He was waiting for her to join him. To begin their first night together.

She turned to her father, urgency coursing in her blood. "Please, Daddy—don't ask me anything now, okay?" She kissed his lean cheek. "I'll tell you everything later."

Looking almost pained with curiosity and anxiety, he stared down at her. "As long as you *are* fine?"

At his worried question, she nodded as her gaze dragged back to Rafael—and her breath caught.

A woman was approaching Rafael—statuesque, flaming red tresses cascading down to her buttocks, dangerous curves in a strapless black dress. She looked as if she was in a trance. Ellie knew that *she* must have looked exactly the same as she'd gravitated toward him hours earlier.

Making a conscious effort to breathe again, Ellie absently answered her father's further demands for assurance, no longer anxious to leave him. She'd better stay put until Rafael sent his admirer on her way.

The woman reached him. Rafael brooded down at her as she talked then he raised his eyes and looked straight at *her*.

After her heart zoomed at the touch of his gaze, it slowed down to a wary rhythm at the emptiness she saw there. Hoping to reestablish the connection meeting his partner and her father had interrupted, she forced a smile only he would understand on her lips.

It faltered when he continued to cast that blank gaze at her. It froze along with her blood as the beautiful redhead put her arm around him and they turned and walked out of the ballroom.

Tremors invading her every muscle, her mind tripped over rationalizations. He must be trying to get rid of that woman without making a scene. When he did, he'd come back. Or not. He expected she'd follow him out. That must have been what he'd been telling her with that vacant stare.

She turned to her father. "See you tomorrow, okay?"

Before he could say anything, she rushed away.

Once outside the ballroom, she felt as if a thundercloud had descended. Then she saw the source of the darkness.

Richard Graves was leaning a formidable shoulder against the gold-paneled wall, watching people like a bored predator deciding which one he'd pick off first, nursing what looked like a straight whiskey. At the sight of her, he lazily unfolded to his full height, making her feel as if the world had shrunk.

Collecting herself, she nodded. "Mr. Graves."

"Looking for Rafael?"

Acutely uncomfortable under his laser gaze, but feeling trapped since she didn't know where to look, she said, "I'll wait until he comes back."

"You'll wait till morning, then. That's the soonest I see him being done with that redheaded ballistic missile."

Her heart boomed painfully. It wasn't *what* he'd said, she told herself. It was Graves himself. She didn't get intimidated easily, but this man—she bet he scared monsters. And for some reason, he'd decided he didn't think much of her.

Not that she cared. She only cared about Rafael's opinion.

"You're mistaken, Mr. Graves. Rafael is..." She couldn't go on. Her throat closed under his pitiless stare and the growing uncertainty and confusion. What *was* Rafael doing?

"Rafael is with—or rather *in*—that redhead now." He had the look of someone taking intense pleasure from pouring acid in an infected wound. "Seems he promised *you* an intensive exercise in his bed, but had a change of plans. Not to mention a huge upgrade in exercise-mat quality. Me, alas, I don't have anything better to do for the night. I might be persuaded to accommodate you in his stead."

She bit her lip to stop it from trembling at his barrage. "Why are you being so...vicious?"

He shrugged. "I'm actually being kind. I'm saving you further embarrassment—if you feel such a thing—and am offering you an alternative, so your night's...efforts aren't a total waste."

Dazed, unable to believe someone would talk to her so offensively, she choked, "I don't know why you disliked me on sight..."

"Instant judgments. And executions. Just two of my many shining qualities."

Corrosive heat surged behind her eyes as she searched his caustic stare. "Are you telling me the truth?"

"That Rafael took that redhead to his quarters and is probably having sex with her as we speak? Yes."

She tore her gaze away, heart flailing as for one last time she silently begged Rafael to come back, prove this cruel man wrong.

But Rafael wouldn't come back.

And every idealistic rationalization was knocked down, replaced with the sordid truth.

Rafael had probably come out to the ball with her because he wanted to see if there was someone who'd appeal to him more before he wasted the night on her. And he *had* found a more beautiful woman, no doubt one who wouldn't dream of asking him to defer his pleasure. And he'd just forgotten about her. He hadn't even deemed her worth another word or glance, as if those hours of magic hadn't happened.

But it hadn't been magic. Not between them. The magic had been all his. A sorcerer casting his dark spells on a willing victim, entertaining himself while he pulled the strings of hundreds of others by remote control.

Graves knocked back the rest of his whiskey before leveling harsh eyes on her. "You're better off. Rafael is way out of your league."

She stared at this man of granite who hacked at her with such pitilessness. But what hurt most was that he was right. About everything.

He rolled his shoulders back, seeming to grow even more menacing as he tossed her a suggestive glance. "I'm even more out of your league, but if you're interested…"

"Enough…*please*."

And she ran away, out of this mansion she'd entered what felt like a lifetime ago, undamaged and oblivious. She now left it with a chasm in her heart, one torn open by the wanton cruelty of the only man she'd ever let her guard down with, the first tears of a deluge scouring down her cheeks.

Ferreira's daughter.

The two words revolved in Rafael's head until he felt it would burst.

He'd lost all sense of time, all sense period, since he'd realized who Eliana was. He'd had to get away before he did something catastrophic. But shock and rage only got more out of control the more they sank their talons in his flesh.

Eliana, the woman he wanted with every fiber of his being, who'd stormed his barriers and brought down his defenses, was the daughter of his slave broker.

Rafael, this is my father, Teobaldo Ferreira.

And he'd once been Rafael's father's best friend and partner.

He remembered all too clearly when Ferreira had been a constant presence in his family's life. Her father hadn't changed much in the twenty-four years since he'd last seen him. As a matter of fact, at sixty-four, he'd aged *very* well. Contrary to Rafael's own father, who'd aged beyond his years. Thanks to Ferreira's heinous crime against him, the man he used to love and trust.

He remembered how *he'd* loved and trusted him. Tio Teo,

he'd called him. His frequent visits had been one of the most anticipated pleasures of the child he'd been.

Then, during his investigations into his abduction, he'd found that just prior to it, his father had dissolved his partnership with Ferreira. Once he'd dug into the events, he'd found conclusive evidence that there had been only one person who could have orchestrated his abduction. Ferreira.

But remembering the man he'd run to greet whenever he'd come visiting, who'd shown him such affection and attention, he'd rejected the evidence, reinvestigated from scratch. He hadn't wanted it to be him. He'd wanted it to be anyone *but* him. But every inquiry had led to the same results. And Ferreira's motivations had been ironclad, too.

Arranging for his abduction would have hit two birds with one stone. Taking revenge on his father, the man he'd publicly accused of destroying him, and accruing enough money to make up for the major losses Ferreira thought he'd caused him. The Organization paid *very* well for their select subjects. He and his brothers had been the most select and costly of their acquisitions. Whoever had sold them had known their worth, had demanded top dollar...and gotten it. In his case, Ferreira.

After he'd gotten conclusive proof, Rafael had concocted the perfect revenge for him. He intended to initiate a real collaboration with him, giving him a taste of the profits and the boost in status, letting his ambitions and greed soar, before he smashed him down from an incredible height. Then he planned to send Ferreira to prison, as he'd sent him. He didn't intend for him to ever get out. Not in this lifetime.

Yet he still hadn't rushed to exact his revenge. The truth was he still struggled with superimposing the image of the monster who'd sold him into slavery onto that of the indulgent uncle he'd loved. He still hadn't relished a face-to-face meeting.

Then he'd seen Eliana and everything but her had ceased

to matter. It was literally the last thing he could have anticipated, for Ferreira to be her father.

A roar tore from his depths.

Something detonated against the wall.

Then the door burst back on its hinges and Richard exploded in, gun drawn and ready to blow any intruder away.

His partner's all-seeing eyes summed up the scene, before tucking his firearm back into the holster at his side. "Redecorating already?"

Rafael turned to where Richard had pointed, staring at the extensive damage to the exquisite plaster wall and the smashed remains of his executive desk and everything that had been on it. He hadn't even thought he could lift it, let alone toss it into the wall. He hadn't gone berserk like that in…ever.

Richard closed the door then approached to circle him. "I thought that redhead would defuse you better than that."

"What redhead?"

"Forgotten her already? You're in worse condition than I thought."

Rafael shook his head, struggling with the adrenaline crashing in his system. He had to get himself under control. Before he had a heart attack.

"How did you find out?" The word Richard had wanted to have with him must have been about Eliana's true identity. Once Ferreira had descended on them, it had become redundant, and he'd left, letting him deal with it on his own.

"About your fantasy girl being Ferreira's daughter? How didn't *you?* Didn't you investigate the man to death? The first thing you must have known about him was his family history."

"I already knew his three sons from his first marriage. The youngest was my age. They were my best friends when we were in and out of each other's homes, even after he divorced their mother two years before my abduction. I found out he remarried right after it and had a daughter with his second wife, who died three years later. So yes, I know everything about him, but I considered the details of his personal life irrelevant to my plans."

"That's the one flaw I see in your plan—that you don't intend to incorporate damages to his personal life."

"His children have nothing to do with his crimes."

"Are you certain about that?"

"I'm certain they had nothing to do with my abduction."

"Becoming tycoons themselves at such a young age suggests they might have shared their father's villainy before each laundered his image and history."

"Like us, you mean?"

"Exactly. Just without our reasons."

Rafael shrugged. "Regardless of any other transgressions they may or may not have committed, I'm only acting as judge, jury and executioner in the crime pertaining to me."

Richard gave a conceding head tilt. "Your prerogative. But you're the man who never misses or forgets a thing, and Eliana isn't a name you hear every day. Didn't it ring a bell?"

A million bells could have rung and he wouldn't have heard them. He'd been that far gone under her spell.

"The only way it didn't is if she gave you a nickname."

"She did, but told me her real name almost at once."

"Did she tell you those as soon as you met?"

"There was no chance for that until much later."

Richard made a satisfied gesture. "There you go."

He frowned. "There I go what? What difference does it make if she told me her name at first or later?"

"Timing is the difference. Later you were submerged under her spell and no longer able to add one and one."

Just what he'd been thinking, even if his view of her spell's nature and Richard's were worlds apart.

"How could you possibly assign devious intent to her actions when this whole thing has been a total coincidence?"

Richard looked at him as if his IQ had dropped a hundred points. "I can because she's Ferreira's daughter, the woman who works with him, and whom he brought here instead of his senior partners to use as bait for you. And it would have worked spectacularly, if not for the tiny detail they're oblivious of—who you really are, and that you're the one reeling him in."

He waved Richard's incriminating theories away. "That's preposterous. You *know* I'm the one who sought her out and that she didn't even know who I was."

Richard's lip curled. "She knew enough about you to cast a spell in your general direction and wait for you to reveal yourself by going after her."

He gaped at him. "You actually believe such nonsense?"

Richard shrugged. "The world, especially this part of it, is full of inexplicable things. Just like this compulsion that came over you when she walked in."

"That's called attraction. That's supposed to be an inexplicable magic, at first at least. Then I touched her, talked to her, and all was explained. To me, she's…perfect."

It was Richard's turn to gape at him. "See that? That's not you talking. I'm starting to think a curse breaker is in order."

"We've progressed from spell to curse? What we shared…"

Richard gave a harsh snort. "Dear Lord—shared? You've had what with that woman? Three, four hours?"

"Time is irrelevant when something is that powerful."

Richard shook his head, regarding him with a mixture of dismay and disparagement. "Seems I'll have to dig deep to find someone who specializes in such potent curses. And there I'd hoped hers was broken when you took off with that redhead. What did you do with her anyway?"

"*What* redhead?"

Richard stared at him. "You really don't remember her?"

Suddenly, he vaguely recalled something. A woman talking while he'd heard nothing but the cacophony of his own thoughts, saw nothing but Eliana across the ballroom. Then the woman was clinging to him and dragging him out of the ballroom. Once outside, he'd shaken her off without a word and stormed to his study from another path that didn't traverse the ballroom.

"No wonder you don't remember that temptress who was wrapped around you. You were still wrapped around Ferreira's daughter's pinkie even as you walked away from her."

It had been the hardest thing he'd ever done. He'd felt as if his heart was being dragged out of his body with every step he took away from her. Then he'd reached the ballroom's threshold and had been unable to go farther. Every cell in his body screamed to get away, but screamed louder to stay close, to not lose sight of her. Everything inside him still rioted, demanding that he return and spirit her away to their promised night....

"Lower the volume, mate." At his start, Richard smirked. "I can hear you thinking of going back for her. But before you go any further down that road, let me underscore that she's the daughter Ferreira lavished his love on while he deprived you of your family and them of you. He sent you to hell where you could have been killed after untold abuse. You can't let that daughter interfere with your revenge on him."

He knew that, but it was all too much to take in....

Richard snapped his fingers. "Snap out of it, mate."

"Get your hand out of my face, *mate*." Suddenly, his fury was back at maximum. "And you actually thought I'd walk away from Eliana and take that woman to bed? Just like that?"

"I would have. But then you're not me. You're no longer you, for that matter." Ice-cold deliberation entered Richard's eyes. "But this Ferreira's-daughter thing *can* work in your favor."

"What the hell do you mean?"

"Think about it. What have you learned about her?"

Rafael glowered at him. If he thought he was going to share anything that had happened between them…

Then he realized. Richard was asking about *Ferreira's* Eliana, not his.

He exhaled heavily, recalling the details he'd archived in his mind as extraneous about Ferreira's then-unknown only daughter. "She was born in the States, and her mother, an Anita Larsen, was an American born to Scandinavian parents." He now understood it was that amalgam of ethnicities that had produced her unique beauty. "Her parents named her Eliana, believing that God had answered their prayers when she was born, after her mother had two early miscarriages…."

He'd said almost the same thing when he'd commented on her name, but hadn't made the connection then when he should have.

Yet, if he had, would it have made a difference? Would he have aborted their intimacies? Could he have? Or had it already been too late from the moment he'd laid eyes on her?

At Richard's go-on gesture, he exhaled again. "She attended university in San Francisco, double majored in business management and child psychology, already has an MBA in the first and is earning another in the second." Which was exactly what she'd told him minus her exact specialties. And he hadn't had a inkling of realization. "But why are you asking? You must have found all this out yourself."

"I did. But you're not mentioning the relevant part. That Ferreira's wife died, leaving him their three-year-old daughter as all that remained of her. That's what makes this such a golden opportunity. Using his daughter against him would make your revenge a hundred times more potent."

Instant abhorrence of the very notion made bile rise to his throat. "If I wanted to involve his family in my revenge,

I would have used his sons. They're the ones who don't see eye to eye with him."

Richard again looked at him as if he feared he had permanent brain damage. "You got that in reverse. Those sons are from a loveless marriage of convenience that imploded after years of cold war. They'd long drifted into their own lives and would make very dull blades. But the daughter he had with the only woman he ever loved—his most beloved person in the world—now, that's a lethal weapon."

"No."

At his adamant rejection, Richard shrugged. "I guess it's just as well you're vetoing the idea. You probably wouldn't be able to use her now, not after you took another woman to bed."

"I did no such thing!"

"Not according to what she now believes."

Rafael gaped at him for long, mute moments. Then he exploded. "*You* made her believe that."

Richard met his apoplectic anger with calm disregard. "When you walked away, I thought your episode of insanity was over and you'd take that woman to bed to cleanse your palate. So when Ferreira's daughter ran out after you, I took it upon myself to make sure she didn't try to insinuate herself under your skin again."

She'd run after him. Even after he'd left her without a word. And Richard had…

"For full disclosure's sake," Richard added, "I also offered to have sex with her in your stead."

The next second, Richard was flat on his back, and Rafael's hand felt broken.

Coming to stand over Richard, who'd pulled himself to his elbows, he growled with rage and pain, "Stay down."

Richard struck out one leg, swiping both of Rafael's from under him. He twisted in midfall, coming down in position to launch into a fight.

Richard did that elastic rebound move that no one his size should be able to do, landing in a crouching stance. The right side of his jaw was already swelling.

"I don't feel like sending you to intensive care, Numbers, but touch me again and I will."

"You can try, bastard."

Richard unfolded to his full height just as Rafael did, his gaze exasperated. "You got it that bad, huh?"

"If you touched her, Cobra, I swear…"

"Please. I just wanted to see how she'd react. She fled from the monster sobbing, predictably." Richard suddenly took him by the shoulders. "You can't let her derail you. Forget her."

"I *can't*. I have to have her. Whatever the cost."

"Even if it is letting her father go unpunished?" Richard asked.

"That's the one thing I won't do for her."

"There's that at least. But you won't even consider that she might have come here with an ulterior motive?"

"No. Besides all evidence to the contrary, I can fathom people."

"Really? Did you fathom her father?"

"I was a child."

"I meant tonight."

Rafael gritted his teeth. He hadn't. Beyond being shocked, beyond knowing Ferreira was a monster, he still hadn't *felt* it.

Richard read his answer in his silence. "You seem to have a serious glitch in your judgment where this family is concerned." A beat. "Did you know that, besides being groomed to be her father's right hand, she does a lot of charity work and volunteering? And that her main focus is orphanages?"

Rafael's heart stopped. Then it boomed out of control.

Unable to bear Richard's presence anymore, he hissed, "Leave."

Richard gave a shrug that said his work here was done then walked away.

At the door he turned, flexing his jaw. "See to that hand. I hope it's broken. It should be a reminder of what this woman has cost you—and will continue to cost you if you don't stay away from her."

Staring after Richard, the pain in his hand throbbed as he stood over the wreckage he'd caused, in the room where he'd found perfection with Eliana. A metaphor for how everything was in ruins at his feet.

Orphanages and helpless children…this was where he couldn't afford rationalizations. That could be too much of a coincidence. And the implications could be…gruesome.

Orphanages were a perfect recruiting ground for the Organization, full of children no one would defend or miss. So had Ferreira found his sale too lucrative? Was he still supplying children? Was she working with him, getting to know those children, to pick the best specimens…?

Deus. He couldn't even contemplate that his Eliana…

But his Eliana might not be real. The only Eliana might be Ferreira's.

If that were true, if everything he'd felt from her was a perfect facade, if she was her father's accomplice, he'd crush both of them to dust beneath his feet.

Five

Ellie felt as if something had been crushed inside her.

She kept pressing her hand to her chest, as if to hold the damaged part back together until it mended. But its sharp edges kept poking into her vitals.

It had been twenty hours since she'd run out of Rafael's mansion at midnight…and yes, the irony wasn't lost on her.

But she was no Cinderella and her prince had turned out to be a predator. As she should have expected, from all the improbabilities.

Ever since she'd fled the scene, she'd been counting the hours. The minutes. Waiting for the misery to subside, for the memory of everything she'd had with him to fade. But time only magnified everything and smashed the broken shards to smaller pieces.

Which was absolutely stupid…and that was precisely what *she* was. Anyone would consider her the dumbest woman on earth if they knew the speed with which and extent to which she'd been bowled over by Rafael. And that she'd gone further, done something she'd never done before. She'd *trusted* him. With her safety, with her heart, with…everything. She'd opened herself so totally, had been so completely unguarded, his unprovoked blow had caused that much damage.

It was pathetic to feel that way when she'd known him only hours. But she'd been so under his spell she'd felt she'd known him forever. Now she knew the truth. What she'd thought a perfect coming together had just been a cheap interlude between a naive moth and a bored flame.

But even knowing that, she hadn't been able to stop crying. When she *never* cried. Tears flowed again every time a memory replayed with such acuteness and clarity. Each look, each touch, each word from him. The man she'd felt so attuned to, so connected to. Who'd turned out to be just another player, only one on a level she hadn't known existed.

Not that that was an excuse. Everything inside her fluctuated from regret for all the beauty that had turned out to be a crude illusion to anger at him for being such a perfect fiend to humiliation that she'd been such an eager mark.

She'd had to run to the bathroom three times while playing with the kids so they wouldn't see her tears. Not that she'd been able to hide her condition from their anxious eyes. But their frantic questions and hugs had made her feel worse, and angry enough at herself to rein in her rampant emotions.

For these orphaned or abandoned children to feel worried and sorry for her when it was they who depended on the goodwill and intermittent care of people like her was a slap that had roused her from wallowing in self-pity.

It also made her knock herself over the head for thinking of canceling her Friday-night entertainment. She wasn't letting a hoarse voice, a puffy face and a broken heart stop her from giving the kids the weekly bedtime performance they'd come to crave over the past month.

She now announced that their entertainment was about to begin, and all the kids ran to their beds excitedly.

They were thirty-six in this ward, from seven to ten years old. She loved all one hundred and twenty kids in Casa do Sol Orphanage, but this ward was extra special and her most enthusiastic audience. And one boy really stood out. She'd clicked with him on so many levels from the first moment, too. But, unlike Rafael, she was sure Diego was who he seemed to be.

The eight-year-old now helped her make a final rundown of her props, put her phone in the portable dock and sound system, then raced back to his bed with a huge smile of anticipation on his face.

Once everyone was in bed, she started performing, complete with dramatic music and on-the-fly costume changes. She always gave them her version of fairy tales, and in this one, Snow White was a Robin Hood–like character with the Seven Dwarves as her swashbuckling sidekicks, and she saved Prince Charming from being turned into a heartless monster by the Evil Queen, who wanted him to be her consort.

Once deep into the story, she forgot everything as she jumped on beds, whirled and swooped and changed voices, wigs and clothes and had the kids kicking in bed with laughter.

"And they lived interestingly ever after."

She took an exaggeratedly deep bow at the kids' fervent applause as the music ended with a flourish.

After stowing all the props in her rolling suitcase, she went from bed to bed kissing and tucking the children in. As usual, she left Diego for last. This time she slipped him the eReader she'd promised him so he could read under the covers. He was The Book Gobbler, one of the things they had in common.

As Diego clung around her neck, he whispered in her

ear, "Will you ask your friend to come a little earlier next time so he can visit us?"

She withdrew to look down at the dark-haired, brown-eyed boy, thinking he'd assigned her an imaginary friend like the one he'd invented for himself. Smiling, she kissed his smooth, olive-skinned cheek. "So what does my friend look like?"

"He looks like a superhero."

"Does he wear a costume and cape?"

"No, he was wearing light blue jeans and a black jacket with a black T-shirt. And his left hand is in a dark blue splint."

Okay. That was pretty detailed. She didn't know Diego had such a knack for dressing his characters.

"That's regular clothes. And the splint is proof he's not invulnerable. So why do you say he looks like a superhero?"

"Because he must be seven feet tall and looks like Batman in his secret identity. He entered in the middle of your story and no one else noticed him. He put a finger on his lips, so I wouldn't interrupt you. Is he your friend or your husband?"

"No one else noticed him, huh…?" The rest caught in her throat, all hairs standing on end. With the relative silence and stillness in the ward, she suddenly felt it. That aura.

She swung her head to the door in time to see a huge shadow separating from the darkness of the entrance vestibule.

Rafael.

Heaving up to her feet, blood didn't follow to her head. She struggled to remain upright as he approached. And he was clapping…albeit with one of his hands in a splint, just as Diego had said.

"That was the best version of *Snow White* I've ever heard. And the most dynamic, entertaining performance I've ever seen. You missed your calling. You should be on stage."

He was dressed as Diego had described. So casually chic and disarmingly handsome it was painful to behold his beauty. And he clearly hadn't shaved since she'd seen him. His beard had turned him from a soul-stealing seducer to a heart-snatching pirate.

"What are you doing here?" she hissed.

Ignoring her anger, he gently swept a finger around one puffy eye and rasped, "I made you cry."

Suppressing a shudder, she stepped away. "I made me cry. But I'm done crying. Answer my question."

Instead of answering, his probing gaze left her to settle on Diego. "Thank you for not drawing attention to my entry and giving me the chance to watch Eliana's performance. Is she always that fantastic?"

Diego nodded enthusiastically. "Always. She's the only one who makes us laugh. And she's the only one who makes me think."

Something scalding came into Rafael's wolf's eyes as they swept to hers. "She's the only one who makes me... do so many things, too." He turned to Diego, extended his hand. "Rafael."

The boy put his small hand in Rafael's with all the decorum of a young prince meeting a vital new ally. "Diego."

A painful tightness gripped her throat as Rafael shook the boy's hand with utmost earnestness. It felt as if she was seeing two versions of Rafael, separated by the chasm of time and circumstance, past and present selves meeting. The way they regarded each other, the awareness in their eyes, as if each recognized something fundamentally the same about the other.

She blinked away the moisture. Where was this coming from? Rafael, the all-powerful tycoon, couldn't have anything in common with an abandoned boy like Diego. Though she knew nothing about Rafael's past, she couldn't imagine he'd ever been as disadvantaged as Diego.

But…what had his childhood been like? How had he become this complex, irresistible force of nature…?

No, Not irresistible. Not to her, not anymore. And she didn't care about his past or present. She didn't want to know anything about him, or have anything to do with him.

"I asked Ellie if she could ask you to come again, just earlier so you could visit us for a while before bedtime."

"It would be a pleasure and an honor, Diego." He slanted her a glance. "*If* Eliana approves."

Ellie tried not to gape at Rafael. It stunned her to see him treat Diego with such respect and regard. Especially after he'd snubbed her father so viciously last night. Before doing the same to her.

"Why do you call her Eliana?" Diego asked. "We all call her Ellie."

"She is Eliana to me. Do you know what that name means?"

Diego shook his head vigorously.

"It means God has answered."

"Answered what?"

"Prayers. So Eliana is God's answer to prayers."

Completely engrossed, Diego probed, "Whose prayers?"

"Her parents. Mine. And I have a feeling yours, too."

Rafael's eyes moved back to her, and the look in them, the way he'd said *mine,* made her forget how last night had ended in humiliation. But that only lasted for moments before she was back to wanting to rant that she never wanted to see him again.

But Diego clung around her neck with even more fervency than usual. "Please, let him come again."

Her fury at Rafael intensified. But she couldn't blast him in front of the starstruck boy, yet she couldn't raise expectations she'd have to disappoint, either.

"We'll see, sweetie. Go to sleep now. Or not."

Forcing a conspiratorial wink, she hugged him one last time and got up before he argued.

Walking away, she struggled not to run out of the ward. It was even worse than she'd thought. All the kids were sitting up in bed, watching Rafael with utmost fascination. They'd never seen anyone like him in their lives. Their interest and eagerness made her curse Rafael even more. Then he made it worse, smiling and waving as he bid them good-night. They all chanted a delighted response.

The moment she closed the door behind them, she turned on him. "What kind of sick game do think you're playing?"

"I never play any kind of game. I'm here to take you with me. I have a promise of untold pleasure to fulfill. And so do you."

"Are you for real? No…don't answer that. Just…"

"Senhor Moreno Salazar!"

She swung around at the excited call and found the nuns who ran the orphanage rushing closer, eyes fixed on Rafael, smiles so large they could have engulfed him whole.

Sister Cecelia, the one who'd called out, started speaking before they reached them. "Now that you've seen Ellie, if you're amenable, we'd love to give you a tour of our orphanage. I know you didn't have a chance to really see the children today, so you won't get an accurate idea of the activities and facilities we have for them, but…"

Rafael waved away her anxious explanations. "I've seen enough. And I already know you're the best since Eliana supports your establishment." He produced a checkbook and pen, scribbled for moments before cutting out a check and handing it to Sister Cecelia. "This is only until you can give me a more comprehensive list of your needs and plans."

The woman took the check dazedly, looking down at it with the other two nuns squeezing closer to get a look, too. Their collective gasps told Ellie it was an obscene amount. At least, to mere mortals. To him, a man who juggled billions, everything was pocket change.

"But…Senhor Moreno Salazar…this is…is…"

"Just something to get you started on those projects you told me you've been forced to put off for lack of funding." He handed her a business card. "These are my personal numbers. Call me when you're ready to discuss your projects in detail. And please, feel free to contact me *anytime* with any problems concerning the children. If you don't have project managers, accountants and attorneys you trust, or if you can't afford any, mine are at your disposal."

The sisters fell over themselves thanking Rafael for his incredible generosity. He waved away their thanks and shook their hands, assuring them he'd make more visits. Then he turned to Ellie, gesturing for her to precede him out of the building.

Feeling as if she'd fallen into another dimension, she walked ahead. Sister Cecelia fell in step beside her. Rafael followed with the other two flanking him.

"Where did you find this angel, Ellie?" Sister Cecelia all but swooned as she kept snatching glances at said angel.

So not even nuns were immune to Rafael's charms. She'd bet nothing that breathed would be.

Biting her tongue so she wouldn't put *fallen* before *angel,* she smiled vaguely, diverting the conversation to weekend plans as they made their way out of the orphanage.

The sisters stood at the door waving and sighing until she and Rafael turned the corner. Once they did, she lengthened her steps, wanting nothing but to escape him.

Without even trying, his longer strides kept him by her side, his imposing figure parting the pedestrians around them on the sidewalk like Moses parted the Red Sea.

Finally, out of breath, she ground to a halt and turned on him. *"What?"*

In answer, he just swept her up in his arms and kissed her.

Just like his first kiss, there were no preliminaries. Just off the deep end into devouring passion. And like they had in that isolated corridor, her senses sang at his feel and taste. The abrasion of his bristling beard and splinted hand stoked the fire that not even his mistreatment had doused, clamoring downtown Rio disappearing around her.

Then the images lodged into her brain. Of him looking at her as if he didn't know her, walking away without a word then disappearing with that woman...

She tore her lips away, struggling until she made him put her back on her feet. But he wouldn't let her escape the cage of his embrace.

She glared up at him. "What was *all* that about? Is making huge, empty promises to vulnerable people the way you get your kicks?"

"I never make empty promises."

"Sure, because you intend to come back to visit an orphaned boy. Because you intend to place all your resources at the disposal of destitute nuns in a backstreet orphanage."

"That's exactly what I will do."

The imperious conviction with which he said that! Last night, she would have believed him without reservations. She would have had as many stars in her eyes as the kids and nuns had when they looked at him. She would have believed him to be the superhero or the angel they believed he was. He'd been even more to her. The sum total of her fantasies. Then he'd walked away and slapped her with the truth. *His* truth.

The horrible part was that even knowing it, she couldn't *feel* it. Let alone see it. He felt and looked sincere and forthright. Not to mention even more gorgeous. The harsh shadows of the beard and what looked like haggardness made him devastating. Even the casual clothes that were nothing like his impeccable attire last night made him more ruggedly sexual. She felt downright dowdy in comparison.

His left arm holding her, the splint digging deliciously into her lower back, he gently swept her bangs away from her eyes. "You were breathtaking in that evening gown. But in this sweater and jeans, with your face scrubbed clean and your hair swinging behind you like a spirited mare's tail, you look even more…edible. And I'm starving for you."

She pushed against him harder, making him release her this time. "How do you do this trick? When you appear to read my mind? It must be your handiest one in getting stupid chicks like me to fall in your arms."

His lips thinned disapprovingly. "First, you're the very opposite of stupid. Second, I'm not interested in 'chicks.' I want only you to fall in my arms. Third, it's not a trick. We are on the same wavelength."

"Yeah, sure. How nice. Well, I can't say it was nice seeing you again. I would have rather broken a toe."

Knowing she sounded childish, she flounced away. He fell into step with her at once.

"Come with me. We need to talk." She turned to blast him and he added, "And to have each other."

His words, his tone painted such erotic images—Ellie winced with longing.

But she needed to settle one thing. "Listen—about that. Thank you for what you did last night. Or what you *didn't* do. Whatever the reason you did pull back, I'm grateful."

He brooded down at her. "I told you why I pulled back."

"Yeah, for me…and all that. I said I don't care why you did it, but I'm thankful anyway. It would have been a far worse mess if you hadn't. But you can drop the act now."

"This is no act."

She exhaled in exasperation. "I don't blame you for walking away, okay? It's what every man should do when he realizes he's dealing with a naive fool who'll be more trouble than she's worth. It's only natural you'd go for the more beautiful, sophisticated woman who actually looks like she's out of her teens, who doesn't say, 'Oops, I didn't meant to go that far that fast,' then ask you to postpone taking your pleasure until she's ready. But what I don't understand is why you're back. If the redhead you spent the night with didn't satisfy you, and you're wishing you'd stuck with your first, if inferior, choice, I'm sorry. My temporary insanity has already lifted."

"I spent the night alone, suffering the most agonizing sustained arousal I've ever experienced. And you were and will remain my only choice. After all, I choose only the absolute best."

God, how did he do this? How did he sound so…convincing?

Wanting to smack herself for wanting to believe him still, she smirked. "A likely story. But whatever the real one is, just leave me alone. As you partner so unkindly pointed out, I'm not in your league."

"Eliana…"

"Taxi!"

She streaked away from his side as the cab she'd yelled for skidded to a halt, as usual barely missing her. Cabdrivers in Brazil had perfected the art of almost hitting their passengers while stopping to pick them up.

Before Rafael could detain her, she'd jumped into the cab, counting on the driver to make it impossible for him to catch up. The driver didn't disappoint her. Even before she told him her address, he screeched away as if to continue a rally race.

She snatched a look backward as they shot through the mayhem that was Rio's evening traffic and saw Rafael standing like a monolith, feet planted apart, hands fisted at his sides, looking the image of volcanic frustration.

Biting down on the urge to yell for the driver to take her back to him, she slumped in her seat. Buckling her seat belt, she tried to let being knocked about by the nerve-racking driving and the subsequent cacophony of horns and road rage distract her.

But his face was all she saw; his taste remained on her tongue, his breath still flaying her cheeks, his hands and hardness imprinted on every inch of her flesh.

She groaned with the severity of the phantom sensations, with craving the real thing. But she'd put an end to any possibility of that. He must have expected she'd fall into his arms again, and now that she hadn't, he'd walk away. For good this time. Which was what she hoped…because any more exposure would compound the damage, scar her permanently.

She suddenly hurtled forward before being brutally yanked back by her seat belt. It took her petrified moments to realize the accident she'd been anticipating hadn't finally happened. It was only the taxi coming to a violent stop in front of her apartment building in Ipanema.

After paying the driver, and thanking him for scaring her enough to take her mind off Rafael, she left the taxi on jellified legs. They hadn't solidified much by the time she entered her one-bedroom apartment on the twenty-sixth floor.

She'd fallen in love with this place the moment she'd seen it. A beachfront unit with wonderful northern exposure, the apartment was high enough to afford her magnificent views of Lagoa Rodrigo de Freitas in daylight, and of the glittering Rio skyline at night.

Finding this place had mitigated her reluctance to be in Brazil. She hadn't wanted to move here, but two months ago, her father had begged her to join him while he pursued the partnership with Rafael. She'd agreed on the condition that she wouldn't stay with him in his villa in Copacabana. He'd been crestfallen, since he'd thought this would be a chance to have her back in his nest after she'd moved out of his Marin County home over a year ago.

Knowing how much he missed being a father hen to her,

she'd almost weakened on the living arrangements. But as long as he had her at home, he was content. She didn't want him content. She wanted him lonely, so he'd do something about the gem he had right under his nose, the gorgeous fifty-two-year-old Isabella Da Costa, who'd been his loyal PA for the past four years.

Whenever she encouraged him, her father reiterated that he was a one-woman man, and he'd lost that woman. And every time she pointed out that twenty years was too long to be alone, he insisted he wasn't alone. He had her. So she made sure he didn't, at least half of the time. Knowing how dependent he was on her for companionship, she hoped it would force him to look for it elsewhere.

But even though she'd been making headway, almost getting him to admit his attraction to Isabella, he kept insisting it wouldn't be fair to a woman to give her less than the whole heart he'd given her mother. But she knew Isabella would settle for *any* corner of his heart, and she was certain that once he left the door to his heart ajar, his smitten PA would take it over completely. He was the most loving man on earth and in time he'd give his all to the woman who loved him.

So here she was, staying out of his way, hoping he'd get it on with Isabella. She wasn't giving up hope. And neither was Isabella.

But up until last night, she'd always felt she was the older one, dealing with an emotionally ambivalent youngster. Being untouched by passion until then had made her coolly cerebral as she sat in judgment, giving sage advice.

Then Rafael had happened.

Now everything she knew about herself and the world had been rewritten, giving her true empathy for her father's turmoil. If only she hadn't had to gain that insight at such a steep price.

Leaning on the door after she closed it, she looked around

the foyer. She'd miss this place. But she'd leave right away. Without telling her father. Once back in San Francisco, she'd explain everything, and that there was no point in him staying in Brazil any longer. Rafael wouldn't give him even the minor business he'd promised her when he'd been having fun at her expense. She'd known mixing sex and business would end badly. She just hadn't thought it would go that bad, that soon.

Exhaling dejectedly, she took off her belt purse as she entered the living room…and almost keeled over in shock.

Rafael was sitting in the middle of the floral couch, his jacket discarded, his T-shirt stretched tautly over his massive chest. From the way his muscled arms were spread over the back of the couch, and those long, powerful legs were stretched out on the coffee table, he looked as if he'd been there for hours.

"How…?"

That was all she could say before she slumped against the wall, not knowing how she remained standing.

He answered her aborted question. "I ran. I took shortcuts that ensured I'd arrive long before your taxi."

"You *ran?*" she choked. "You're not even out of breath."

"I'm in very, very good shape."

He could say this again. Her gaze slid hungrily over his body before it faltered, stopped then slammed up back to his as she burst out, "How did you enter my apartment?"

"My background in crime is very, very handy."

So that had been true. He'd once been a gang member… or worse. Which did explain that lethal edge to him. She wondered how deadly he had been. Or still was. She also wondered why she wasn't in the least afraid of him. His presence here didn't frighten or even alarm her. It just annoyed her. And if she was totally truthful…thrilled her.

But then he just had to exist to do that. Even now…

Exasperated with herself more than him, she harrumphed. "That's all you have to say? You used your criminal creds to con your way past the concierge, then to pick my locks?"

He inclined his head in utmost tranquility. "Yes."

"Well, marathon man, you can run out the same way you ran in. I have nothing more to say to you."

He spread himself out even more comfortably. "But I have something to say to you. I realized I missed telling you the one relevant thing—why I walked away."

She teetered away from the wall's support but found her legs were still rubbery. "You found a woman that appealed to you more."

"As I said before, no woman has or will ever appeal to me more than you...."

"Oh, *please.*"

He heaved up from his deceptively relaxed pose and in three endless strides was, like last night, plastering her against the wall. "That's all I aim to do—all I will do—please you. And pleasure you and cater to your every need."

"Rafael..."

He clamped his mouth over hers, swallowed her gasp and plunged deep. Delight went off like fireworks through every nerve ending as his hard length impacted her, as his tongue thrust into her recesses, all mental faculties shutting down.

It was he who finally raised his head, cradling hers in the crook of his arm, his eyes endless silvered twilights.

Then he took her hand, lying limply over his chest, and guided it down. Her gaze followed, her whole body lurching as he placed it over the huge hardness tenting his pants.

"You feel this? See it? That was how obviously turned on I was as I took you into the ballroom last night."

She hadn't noticed, because she'd been too busy looking for her father. But she did remember how his arousal had remained blatantly apparent through the more relaxed suit pants all the time in his study.

"I didn't care who saw it. But not even finding myself faced with your father...deflated me. I didn't want to get introduced to a man I'll work with in that state—especially when said man happens to be your father. I didn't know how to handle it so I walked away. It was immature and tactless, but once it was done, I didn't know how to undo it." His lips hovered over hers and his breath singed her face. "I waited for you to come to me, so you'd advise me how to fix my faux pas. But you didn't."

"So you left with another woman." She moaned as he bent his knees to thrust against the junction of her thighs.

"I didn't. When she steered me outside I just kept going until I went back to our place. I thought you'd rejoin me. When you didn't, I thought you'd gotten angry and left and thought it was just as well. If you'd come back, I would have taken you right there and then. Ever since, I've been investigating you."

She finally ducked out of the prison of his seduction. "I thought my details didn't matter."

"They didn't, until I had to find you. But I learned so much more about you being in your home."

Embarrassment suddenly struck her at having this immaculate entity in her messy abode. "It's a rental. But it sure must be a novelty for you, being in a packrat's place."

His lips crooked in a smile of such indulgence. "You are a collector, aren't you? But since this isn't one of your permanent homes, it means you travel with your mementos."

"Yeah, I unpack them first thing and have them covering every available surface and hanging on every wall as soon as I get anywhere I intend to stay longer than a month. And tidy is something no one could accuse me of being...."

He covered the distance she'd put between them, pulling her back into his arms. "I love your mess. I've had painstaking order my whole life. Anywhere I lived was minimalist. I do everything according to sparse equations. Then I entered your home and it was as if a warm breeze swept over me, dispelling the cold I carry within me. Everything here tells a meticulously detailed story of who you are, who you love, what matters to you. And it's just exquisite. Like you."

The barrage of beauty spilling from him had her dissolving in his arms. "God, where did you learn to...*talk* that way?"

"I never did. It just comes out of me when I'm with you. And I need you to be as spontaneous with me. I can't bear the walls you've erected between us. I need your passion-hued eyes to melt me with your all-out appreciation again."

"Passion-hued..." she repeated on a sigh.

He *was* too much. And she wanted him too fiercely.

She sighed again. "Okay. Let's do it."

Confusion crept into his eyes. "Do what?"

"Have sex."

Six

"I assume you have protection this time?"

Rafael disengaged from Eliana with the same caution he would distance himself from a bomb.

Just as guardedly, he said, "I don't."

"There's a pharmacy nearby that delivers merchandise," she murmured.

He shook his head, as if it would change what he was hearing. "What's come over you?"

She raised one eyebrow challengingly. "That's why you're here, right? The untold pleasure thing you said we promised each other? So let's cut the chase."

"You mean cut to the chase."

"No, I mean what I said. You seem to want me the more I resist, so I'm ending the chase. Let's do it."

"Stop saying *it*."

"What do you want me to call sex?"

"Don't say that, either. When I take you it won't be 'sex.'"

"You like to refer to it as 'making love'?"

"I never 'refer to it' as anything."

"You just do it, huh? Fine by me."

"I said stop it, Eliana." He scowled at her, but those eyes of hers were unrepentant. And they inflamed him even more for it. His lips twitched. "But if I must give what we'll share a name, it would be something like…plunging in passion."

The twist of her lips told him what she thought of his flowery descriptions. He couldn't fault her ridicule. He was stunned at what kept spilling from his lips himself.

He exhaled forcibly when she kept looking stubbornly at him. "Why the sudden change of mind?"

She shrugged. "I doubt I'll ever want a man like I want you, and you want to have sex—oh, sorry—to *plunge in passion* with me. Probably to uphold your record of never having a woman say no to you. But I no longer care about your motive. I just want to find out what the fuss is all about. Once you're appeased, you'll walk away again and that will be that."

"First, I don't have a record. Second, I didn't walk away in the first place."

"So you say."

"So you didn't believe my explanations?"

"They're no longer relevant. So if you want to take me to bed, I want that, too. But let's be clear about what it will be—a one-night stand or at most a very brief liaison."

His insides tightened. This was spiraling out of control, going where he never expected. "Is this what you want?"

Another shrug. "This is what will happen."

"Is this about my wealth and power again?"

"It's about everything that you are. I always held my own with anyone, but I can't with you. You are *way* out of my league."

"Stop saying that, too," he growled, exasperation soaring.

"It's the truth, as your horror of a friend said."

"Seems he has more than I thought to answer for."

"He just pointed out what I was trying not to see so I can have some time with you. But I need balance in any relationship, no matter how fleeting, and the gross imbalance of power between us is something I can't deal with."

He reached for her hands carefully, as if afraid she'd bolt away and never let him near again. "Those tiny hands turn me to mush. I am powerless where you're concerned. And since you're the one who has the will to resist me, that makes you the one with the power in this relationship."

She snatched her hands away, hugging herself in a defensive gesture. "We don't have a 'relationship.' And if you haven't noticed, that will to resist you lasted about an hour. So here I am...offering myself like I did last night. But this time I know what to expect. So take me or leave me. Your choice."

Frustration boiled over at her finality, which he knew in his bones was no act. "You believed me last night without reservations. Why do you doubt everything I say now?"

Her shoulders jerked on what felt like dejection. Then she kicked off her sneakers and sat down on the armchair by the couch, curling her legs beneath her.

She looked so small and vulnerable, nothing like the entity who'd sizzled with energy and enchantment as she'd entertained the children. Yet she was the most formidable force he'd ever encountered. Her hold on him was growing by the second. He suspected it might already be unbreakable.

She sighed. "Something changed when you walked away. And I guess I...woke up. I did try to cling to the fantasy, but you and your partner thankfully made it impossible. So though your explanation is so lame it should be true, since you could have come up with something better if you were lying, it doesn't revive the trust I felt in you. You're no longer the man I trusted implicitly, just another person I have to take my usual precautions with. That's why I need the upfront terms to guarantee I won't end up feeling like I did last night."

And *that* was where he'd miscalculated. He'd come here counting on that trust to make his justifications readily acceptable to her but hadn't realized he'd already pulverized it. And that her being so in tune with him would actually backfire. She now saw through the fakeness of his explanations, just as she had sensed the truth of his every word and emotion last night.

So he didn't deserve her trust, not where her father was concerned, but he'd meant every word he'd said to her—and about her. And now that he'd made sure her orphanage work was all benevolence, he was free to surrender to what he felt for her.

How this would work in tandem with his revenge on Ferreira, he had no idea. And for now, he didn't care. He just needed her trust and spontaneity back.

And he would do *anything* to have all of her again.

He crouched down beside her armchair, struggling not to haul her out of it and crush her in his arms. "Then give me a chance to take you back to the fantasy and I will make it a reality. I will erase the change that happened inside you."

She curled tighter, like a cat shying away from petting. "The change I felt happened inside *you*. I can't explain it, but it...hurt."

Had she felt his hatred and aggression when he'd seen her father, and it had pained her that much? She was *that* supremely sensitive to everything he felt?

"I know I didn't know you long enough to have the right to feel or say any of that..."

He took the hands twisting on her lap to his aching lips. "You have every right to feel and say anything. We already agreed what we share transcends time."

"I agreed to that when I was still under your spell."

"Then let me cast another one."

She wrenched her hands out of his. "No thanks. Sex is all I want from you now, all I have to offer. If you want to play more games, I'm no longer available for those."

"No games, Eliana. Never any games. This is deadly serious to me." He succumbed to the need to wrap his arms around her, laid his head on her breasts, listening to the music of her heartbeats. "I spent the night in a fever, my mind flooding with images and sensations. Of silk sheets drenched in your sweat, of your hot velvet limbs around me, of your cries rising in the dark."

The heart beneath his ear raced, with his every word, but when she talked her voice was as stiff as her body. "No need to fantasize anymore. Take me and be done with it."

He withdrew instead. This wasn't how he wanted her. And then there was something else.

"You said something earlier…about finding out what the fuss is all about. Did you mean me or sex in general?"

"I meant sex with you. After all the buildup, I'm warning you I have ginormous expectations."

"I will provide you with satisfaction of massive proportions." He took her hands in his good one. "But there's one thing I need to know. Are you a virgin?"

"Are you going to have sex with me now?"

He growled at the word *sex*. "No."

"Well, when you decide to make good on your promises, I'll let you know. Until then, that's privileged info." Her fiery eyes crackled with ire. "What's it to you anyway?"

"Just finding out my variables. If you're a virgin, I'll live with it. If you're not…I'll also live with it."

"Both variables sound equally unwelcome to you. Which is hard luck for you, since these are the only two available."

He stroked a finger down her hot cheek, loving the way it trembled at his touch. "I actually welcome either. I would just appreciate a heads-up as to which is the truth, as it would dictate my…approach."

Scoffing and choking on mortification at once, her eyes and lips became petulant. "Then why won't you take me to bed now and end the suspense once and for all?"

"Because I made a promise to you that I would take it slow."

"But I'm telling you I no longer want slow."

"Only because you want to punish me."

This time her scoff was pure derision. "Gee, I didn't realize taking me to bed would be such a hardship."

"You can't forgive me, so you want to have me so you can get me out of your system and get rid of me. Just wanting this is as harsh a punishment as you can deal me." Releasing her tresses from the elastic band, his groan echoed her moan as he massaged her scalp, sealed her lips with his and poured his pledge into her. "But I'm in your system to stay, *minha* Eliana."

The way she melted into his kiss—like all the parts of him he hadn't known had been missing fitting back into his being—made his head spin with hunger.

Before he forgot all the big talk about not taking her now, he released her.

She gasped, "I—I do forgive you."

His heart thundered. "You do?"

"For last night. But I can't forgive you for today."

"You mean showing up uninvited at the orphanage? Attending your performance without your consent?"

She pushed at him, furious tears surging in her eyes. "How about dangling yourself in front of those deprived kids, especially a boy like Diego? He is *starved* for an adult male presence in his life. Then you appear like a genie that could grant him his every wish, treating him as if he mattered to you and making idle promises. Didn't you think you'd be adding another letdown to a lifetime defined by abandonment?"

The lash of her disapproval felt like salt in every open wound. "I meant every promise I made to him."

She jumped to her feet, glared down at him. "That you'd visit him? Once? More? Then what? Don't you realize the hopes he could be pinning on you? And that he's already hero-worshipping you?"

He rose to his feet, met her glare with his. "Are you telling me not to see him again?"

"I'm telling you it's dangerous, it's thoughtless and it could end up damaging him. I saw his expectations soar just realizing you exist, and when you showed him interest and regard, it developed into a tangled mess right before my eyes. A fall from such heights back to the bleakness of his reality would be devastating."

She had a point. No matter that this boy so reminded him of himself at the age when he'd also found himself without a family, he had to tread carefully. He'd felt an incredible connection with Diego on sight, almost as strong as the one he'd felt with her. And although he *did* have intentions he would see through, he didn't have a clear-cut plan in place yet. So for now, he just sighed, nodded in concession.

Taking this to mean he wouldn't pursue the matter further, she exhaled. "About the check you cut to the orphanage—care to give me a number? Just so I know how bad the heart attack you gave the sisters was?"

"A million dollars." At her gasp, he elaborated, "I estimated it's what they need for immediate needs, and for rebuilding the parts of their convent and the orphanage that got damaged in the last tropical storm. But once they give me a comprehensive list of what they need for the children I'll provide them with open funding."

She gaped at him. Then she swallowed. "Thank you."

He bent and caught the convulsive movement in her throat in an openmouthed kiss. He really couldn't keep his hands and lips off her for longer than a few minutes. "Thank *you*."

Throwing her head back, giving him license to worship her, she moaned, "Thank me for what?"

He raised his head. "For guiding me to Casa do Sol. My aid work is focused on organizations for children, but so many are inferior hellholes while others use children to bait donations that end up lining the pockets of the managers. I always have to deal with inefficiency or crush corruption before I can benefit the children. When I found you've been mostly working with Casa do Sol since you came to Rio, I investigated and found out that it's the one orphanage that's above all suspicion, as well as the one offering their children the best quality of life. That's why I wrote them a check on the spot."

That appreciation he was already addicted to was back in her eyes. Now it mixed with bashfulness. "That was very... thorough of you. Not to mention very thoughtful."

"It's just a start. If you have any ideas for improving the orphanage, or specific wishes for the children, make me a list. I will make them all a reality."

"Thank you, I will." She suddenly hid her face in his chest, peach staining her cheeks. "I didn't know you had such an ongoing involvement in helping children. I'm sorry I accused you of being oblivious to their needs."

A finger below her chin raised her eyes to his. "You were looking out for the children's best interests."

"I shouldn't have interpreted your actions in the worst way just because I was angry with you. I'm really sorry."

The whole world darkened as her eyes filled. She was that upset she'd misjudged him.

He hugged her fiercely, needing to absorb her dismay. "I *am* too powerful, and your worry that I might thoughtlessly step over the vulnerable without noticing was well founded. You couldn't know what I do as I keep those activities a secret."

She buried her face in him again, shaking her head. "I still shouldn't have jumped to conclusions."

He tilted her chin up again. "You're painfully fair. I love this about you, as long as the pain you inflict in your fairness isn't on yourself."

"You don't mind if I inflict it on you?"

"I welcome anything you inflict on me. I invite it." A deep drugging kiss. "I beg for it."

After he let go of her lips, she let out a crystalline laugh. "Diego read you right on the spot, too. He said you looked like Batman in his secret identity. That guy is also a billionaire philanthropist."

"With the difference that Bruce Wayne advertises his philanthropy. I can't even bear the word."

Her eyes grew thoughtful, the warmth he'd been sorely missing flooding back in them. "So you don't like considering what you do philanthropy?"

"I just have the means to achieve things. So I do."

"And you hide your altruism while you leak info about a criminal past and affiliations. You want the world to learn about your lethal edge but not your gooey center, huh?"

He swung her around to her squealing delight, grinned down widely at her. "See? You read me like no one ever has." Putting her back on her feet, he probed, "But how did *you* know about Casa do Sol? Did you investigate them, too?"

"No. I just made visits everywhere, and they were the only ones I felt…good about."

"So again your instincts proved infallible. You read everyone, not just me. It's *your* superpower."

"It never felt like a good thing. It leaves me with precious few people in my life."

"You only need a few who *are* precious." He squeezed her tighter. "Though I'd rather you only need me."

The flush that flooded her face was adorable. Before he commented on her paradoxical shyness—given that she hadn't batted an eye while asking him to have sex—he realized his hand was hurting like hell. He'd been using it as if nothing was wrong with it.

He raised it up. "Aren't you going to ask about my hand?"

A stubborn look came into her eyes. "No."

"You don't care that I broke it?"

"Are you going to take me now?"

"No."

"Then I don't care."

He guffawed as she stuck her nose up at him. He'd never laughed that way, so elated and unfettered.

Still laughing, he swept her up, and his heart boomed at the way she clung to him, fitting into his every emptiness. The memory of her earlier rejection jolted through him, making him gather her tighter. He was never letting her recede from him again.

In her bedroom, another place full of her mementos, he laid her down on the burgundy comforter and came down half over her. She wriggled beneath him until she'd brought him fully over her, pulling him into an all-body hug.

He rose on one arm, the pain in his loins becoming agony. "You'll blow all my fuses."

She arched up into him. "Serves you right."

"It wouldn't serve *you* right."

She giggled, clung harder and brought him down between her thighs.

He groaned. "I was right. You are an enchantress."

"I was wrong. You're not a sorcerer. That sort of implies a level of benevolence. You're pure evil."

At once laughing at her pout and grunting in pain, he rolled off her. It was unheard of for him to defer having anything he wanted. But doing so with her was the most pleasurable thing he'd ever experienced.

If anyone had told him last night he'd be lying side by side with her in her bed, just to hold her and talk, when he'd never hungered for anything as much as he hungered for her, he would have thought them insane. But now, he couldn't imagine anything better as she slipped her limbs into the exact places where he needed them, holding on with the exact intensity he craved.

Sighing after she'd settled into him as if she'd been doing so all their lives, he reached over her and picked a frame off her crowded bedside table.

The photo was of a woman and a little girl, both grinning unreservedly at the photographer, throwing their arms wide as if to embrace him and the life they loved with him. The object of their all-out affection was obviously her father.

A pang twisted in his gut at yet another proof of the depth of emotions she had for that man.

Banishing Ferreira from his thoughts, he focused on this piece of her past, another detail bringing him closer to her.

"You got a lot from her."

She nodded, threading her fingers through his hair. "I also got a lot from my father."

After seeing them together, he hated to admit that was true. But then, on the outside, the man was a perfect specimen. Rafael was certain that on the inside Eliana hadn't been tainted by any trace of his weaknesses and evils.

"Whatever you got, wherever you got it, you became this one-of-a-kind amalgam."

She gave an adorable little snort. "Did you go to the University of Extravagant Descriptions? Then got a PhD in hyperbolic metaphors?"

"Hush. I have all that vocabulary that I never found use for. You're getting the benefit of it all."

"Whether I like it or not, huh?"

He tugged a thick tress. "Oh, you like it."

A sigh clasped her even closer against him. "Yes."

He kissed her forehead. "Do you remember her?"

Her eyes became suddenly turbid. "Everyone thinks that I couldn't possibly remember all that I do about her, since I was just three when she died, and that what I think are my memories are just from what Daddy kept telling me about her as I grew up. But I do remember her. Very well. Too well sometimes."

He feathered kisses all over her face, needing to take away the raw edge of memories. "Is this why you give so much of your life to orphans?" Almost every weekend, and after work almost every day. "Because you feel like one, and you feel her loss so keenly?"

"If I feel that way when I have the best father in the world, I can't imagine how those who've lost both parents, or never had anyone feel."

The best father in the world. The man who'd sent him to hell. But she had nothing to do with his crimes. And he'd keep her away from their fallout, whatever it took.

He forced down the bile that rose to his mouth. "Next time I see Sister Cecelia I'll correct her. *You're* the angel."

Her eyes widened. "You heard her?"

"I have very, very good hearing."

Her eyes grew heavy as they traveled down his body. "Everything about you is very, *very good.*"

He caught her tongue in a gentle bite, sucked it inside his mouth. "I'm agonizingly thrilled you approve...as you can feel."

He ground his hardness against her and she mewled, became even more pliant against him. His head almost burst with the urge to forget his promise and just take her as she'd asked. But he had to wait. Had to deepen her involvement until she was as dependent on him as he was on her.

Insinuating a leg between his, she pressed her knee into his erection, wringing a growling thrust from him.

She chuckled, eyes telling him she considered them equal now. "But Sister Cecelia got it right, even if at the time I wanted to tell her that fallen angel would describe you better."

"It would. I've done very, very bad things in my time. I still do, when the need arises."

Her eyes grew serious. "But not to innocents."

It was a statement, not a question. Pride expanded inside him that she trusted him again, and saw his fundamental truth.

"No. But the law still calls what I did and do illegal."

"The right thing to do isn't always legal. And as long as no innocents were harmed, as long as you help them like when you crush those corrupt people to save helpless children, then *I* call what you do heroic." She sighed wistfully. "Sometimes I wish I could do the same, but I don't have enough power. I'm only thankful someone like you who does exists, and that you use your power this way."

Was it possible that once he destroyed her father—if she ever realized it was him who did it and she found out the reasons why—she'd find his actions heroic? At least, excusable and understandable?

"You can't imagine how helpless I feel most of the time." Her pain made him want to go out destroying everything that had ever made her feel this way. "I try to reach out to as many children as I can—to provide them with someone who cares, who's there to listen to their problems and ideas, to take part in their activities, to encourage their interests and talents. But no matter how hard I try, I always feel nothing I do is enough. Thank God for people like the sisters who do far more. But someone like you? You can do the most."

His throat tightened. "What you do will make a difference in those children's psyches. I just throw my money and weight around, but I never made a child's day better in person. Truth is, I never even interacted with one, until Diego today."

"But without your 'money and weight,' we wouldn't have the places and projects to offer any children anything."

"So we complement each other." She snuggled deeper into his chest, nodded. "We already knew that, just not how completely we do."

Raising her face, her smile and gaze caressed him. "But you must now know everything about me since I sprouted my first baby teeth. And I know nothing about you."

He rose on one elbow. "What do you need to know?"

"Tell me about your family."

He'd been prepared with a fabricated history. But he couldn't bear more lies between them than necessary. He'd tell her the truth—a carefully edited version of it.

"My parents divorced when I was ten. My mother remarried two years later and had three more children, two girls and a boy. My father remarried much later, and had two children, a girl and a boy. I exited their lives early and never reentered it. I sort of watch them from afar, keep my distance."

"Is this what you want?"

"With my kind of life, with what I've been involved in, they were better off with me as far away as possible. When it became feasible for me to approach again, I still felt it wasn't in their best interests for me to disrupt their lives."

"How can you say that? I'm certain they'd love to have you be an integral part of their lives."

He tickled her, trying to inject lightness into what was suddenly oppressively serious. "Who's being biased?"

She grinned impishly, then turned back to seriousness

at once. "But I really do imagine they would choose to be as close as possible to you if you gave them the choice."

The talons in his throat sank a little deeper at her conviction. "It's a bit more complicated than that."

He expected her to probe this vagueness, but she only exhaled. "As long as you're sure that it's for the best. But even if it is, I still hate to think you've exiled yourself from your family. That you've chosen to be alone."

"I'm not alone. I'm part of a...brotherhood, if you will."

"One of them is that terror you have for a partner, huh?"

He guffawed at her wary-feline expression. "He was an addition to our brotherhood. He used to be my mentor."

"He thinks he's your father. Or your 'Big Brother.'"

He laughed harder as she made the quotes gesture. "You're uncanny. You analyze everything with such absolute accuracy."

"He didn't need analysis. He knocked me over the head with his 'shining qualities.'" Another quote gesture.

"I assure you he hasn't gotten *and* won't get away with it. But speaking of family...I insulted your father almost as much as Richard did you."

"Oh, no, there's just no comparison. My father almost didn't notice you, as anxious as he was about me."

"I would still like to apologize. Will you please set up a proper meeting?"

A still look came into her eyes. "You want to meet him... as my father or as a potential partner?"

"Can't I meet him as both?"

She grimaced. "You know where I stand on this issue."

"Why don't you let me handle this?"

"I've never been as miserable as I was last night, and I don't want to risk something like that happening again."

"It won't. I promise."

The troubled look that gripped her face almost made him

tell her to forget it. But before he could say anything, she nodded, then nestled back into him.

As he received her into his embrace, that trust he craved, which she was bestowing on him in full again, weighed on him. It didn't feel like a privilege anymore but a responsibility.

One he ultimately had to betray.

Seven

The meeting with Ferreira took place the very next afternoon. During lunch hour so it would be brief, at Eliana's request.

Rafael picked Casa de Feijoada, a busy spot in the posh beachside Ipanema district, a mile away from Eliana's place, and Ferreira's offices, for their convenience. The restaurant was cozy, with a tropical, rattan-walled look and family-style table service. He came a bit early to arrange a table on the beach and order the lunch courses in advance so no unnecessary delays would occur during their hour-long meeting. They arrived at one o'clock sharp, and Eliana greeted him with the same ardent kiss with which she'd said good-bye when he'd left her apartment at 2:00 a.m.

Though she'd confided that she'd told her father everything, so he must have an idea how things stood between them, he glimpsed a spurt of anxiety in Ferreira's eyes as he witnessed that intimacy. But like the gentleman everyone believed him to be, the impeccably dressed and behaved

Ferreira made no comment. Not on that nor on Rafael's offensive behavior during the last ball, nor his no-shows in the previous ones.

From then on, they settled down to the smooth flowing lunch courses. Apart from the effort Rafael expended to sit across from Ferreira—the man he'd once loved as an uncle and who'd betrayed him in the most unspeakable way—pretending this was their first real meeting, nothing of note happened.

Ironically, the man who'd been trying to meet him for the past two months didn't seem to care that Rafael possibly held his professional future in his hands, only that he might affect his daughter's adversely. Ferreira spent the entire lunch watching them interact, saying little. He never once broached the subject of the partnership. The only questions her father asked him were when Eliana went to the ladies' room: oblique ones probing his intentions and warning him against toying with her. In turn, Rafael as indirectly let Ferreira know that where Eliana was concerned, they were on the same page. She came first to him, too.

That seemed to disturb Ferreira instead of reassure him. He considered Rafael's statement an exaggeration, since the sum total of their liaison had taken place over three days. But when Rafael told him that the power of their connection had dispensed with the usual stages needed to reach their current level of involvement, Ferreira finally relaxed. Though he'd evidently never thought Rafael was capable of forging such a connection, from what he'd heard about him, he confessed that he knew how it could be that way from intimate experience. It had been the same between him and Eliana's mother. They'd married a week after meeting and had lived ecstatically ever after—until aggressive pancreatic cancer had taken her from him.

On Eliana's return, the conversation turned to anecdotes about Eliana's mother, and her half brothers and their mother. Ferreira had had two extreme opposites in the marriage department. The first one when his father had arranged his marriage to his partner's daughter and the battlefield that marriage had turned into. Then the marriage to the love of his life, which had started with love at first sight and had ended with him living in her memory and for their daughter.

The lunch ran thirty minutes longer than the agreed on hour before Ferreira rose to leave. As Rafael shook his hand, the man gave him a pointed look. *Don't hurt my daughter* was the gist of the volumes it spoke. His answering look said *I would* never *hurt her.* He hoped the *but I'll hurt you... bad* part went unsaid.

The moment her father disappeared, Eliana dragged Rafael by his tie and planted a hot kiss on his lips.

Starving for her already, he moved to deepen it, and she pulled away, chuckling, eyes heavy with hunger. "I shouldn't be kissing you after I just binged on that *feijoada.* Rinsing my mouth can't begin to counteract its garlicky goodness."

Brazil's national dish was indeed an antisocial stew. This restaurant that proclaimed itself the meal's house was lauded by Cariocas, Rio's residents, as serving the best *feijoada* in Rio. Even after he'd ordered their best meal, he hadn't expected the giant pot of meats swimming in saucy black beans they'd gotten. The tureen had been piled high with smoked and peppery sausages, *carne seca* ham and an assortment of other pork cuts. He was glad he remembered to tell them not to serve the pig's ears, tail and tongue.

He pulled her back against him, claiming her lips. "Having binged on the same pungent bomb, all I taste is your sweetness." Another savoring kiss. "And the tartness of acai and *maracuja* and dragon fruit from that Amazonian fruit smoothie."

She suddenly yelped, pulling back once again. "You always scorch me, but now you literally do. Those deadly *malagueta* peppers you gobbled are still lacing your lips and tongue." Licking the burning away, she smiled. "Thank you."

He pressed his lips as if to secure her kisses there. "What for?"

"For being so nice to my father."

"He's a nice man."

He didn't even have to lie. Apart from the sadness he glimpsed in Ferreira's eyes—which Eliana said had been there since her mother's death—and his wariness of how the power Rafael wielded would affect his daughter's well-being, Ferreira was apparently the kind and agreeable man he remembered. The evil he'd committed against him had carved no visible telltale signs on his visage.

Eliana sighed. "I actually think you didn't like him much, but you were still extremely nice to him. So thank you."

Deus. Those instincts of hers continued to prove sharper than he'd even thought. He'd thought he'd been seamless.

Before he could say something to alleviate her suspicion, she added, "But it's expected on a first meeting with my wary father hen. He spent lunch watching your every move. And you're a man who suffers no monitoring or judgment."

Relieved she'd found a benign reason for the hostility she'd felt from him, he exhaled. "It's only natural he'd be worried about how fast things developed between us. I think I ended up allaying his anxiety."

"I know." She smiled up at the waitress, who put the bill before him. "Why do you think I went to the ladies' room?"

"And there I thought you didn't have a wily bone in your body." He grinned as he got out his credit card.

She chuckled. "No wiliness involved, I assure you. I was instructed to do so. On the way, Daddy begged me to give him any chance to be alone with you. He claimed there was no way he could 'read' you as long as I was around. He also begged me not to be my shockingly candid self while he's around." She shot him a devilish look. "I did manage not to say things like, 'Don't worry about Rafael seducing me, Daddy. I spent a whole night slithering all over him and begging him to have sex with me, and he was the one who held back and reprimanded me about my language, too!'"

Rafael threw his head back on a guffaw. "It's a good thing you exercised some self-control. You would have given him a heart attack."

Her laugh tinkled like crystal. "I did give him a minor one with that kiss when we first came in. The poor man always bragged he was the only man he knew whose daughter never gave him any nightmares about boyfriends, since I never had any. Then I go and get all mixed up with someone who's as much trouble as ten thousand men put together."

"So I'm all his postponed nightmares come all at once."

And she didn't know how literally true that was.

"Exactly." She laughed, her gemlike eyes radiating mischief and joy in Rio's midday sun. Entranced as he gazed into them, he threw some bills down, and she giggled harder. "That tip could make you a partner in this restaurant."

"The food and service were impeccable. They earned it."

"It *was* lovely. But then it didn't have to be. Just being with you would make anything wonderful."

He knew she meant every word. She was the first woman, the first person, who'd ever told him everything she felt, no games. And it was intoxicating.

"I also want to thank you for not talking business."

"I want to discuss a few things with you before I bring up anything with him. I have reports, but I want what only an insider would know."

"Let it go altogether, okay? Even my father didn't bring up business. Now that he saw us together, I believe he won't."

"I know he has big problems, Eliana."

Dismay flooded her eyes. "I guess it was too much to hope that you of all people wouldn't find out. But we're working on a resolution, and I'm hopeful we'll soon have it."

"I know a partnership with me would help resurrect his business. Even if I don't give it to him, I still want to help." He did intend to save her father's business, for her, to preserve her legacy. He'd seen Ferreira's will, and she was his only beneficiary. No matter what he felt about her father, he wouldn't let her inherit an ailing enterprise. He buried his lips in her palm. "Let me help."

She caressed his cheek, hand trembling as it was singed by his passion, her gaze softening with gratitude. "It doesn't matter if you can help, it's enough you want to."

"I can do anything, remember?"

"Oh, yes, you can." Her smile was tenderness itself. Then suddenly she pushed her chair back and stood up.

He rose at once. "Where are you going?"

"Back to work. Then to the orphanage." She grinned as she reached for her coat. "As you already know."

He helped her on with the coat that matched the deep royal-blue dress he'd spent much of the lunch hour fantasizing about ripping off her.

She hooked her purse across her body. "See you at my place later? Or would you rather I come to yours?"

"I'll come to you. And I don't want you driving on that road alone again, so whenever you want to come to my place, I'll pick you up. Eight o'clock?"

"Make it nine." Her smile lit up the whole world as she walked into his arms and met him halfway in a kiss that had the whole restaurant watching.

After she left, some men gave him the thumbs-up. One was giving him two.

Mock bowing to them, he walked out into the hubbub of Rio's midday congestion. Cariocas filled the streets as they did every hour of the day. Anyone coming to Rio came for its laid-back beach culture as much as its breathtaking landscapes and abundant tourist attractions. And everyone got the impression the Cariocas were on perpetual vacation.

He breathed deep of the ocean breeze and the unique scents of this city he'd spent his formative years in. It was strange how alien he felt here. His kidnapping had truly cut all the ties he had with his past, with the being he'd been.

But Rio was still the place he'd been taken from, and it was where he'd returned to enact the vengeance he'd waited for almost a quarter of a century. Three quarters of his life.

Then in three days, Eliana had turned his world upside down and shifted his priorities.

But his plans were only postponed, not cancelled. He would still punish her father.

Just not before he secured her.

At eight o'clock sharp, that Amazonian parrot she had for a bell burst into song.

Ellie flew to the door, heart soaring as she snatched it open, expecting to see Rafael. He was there. Only not alone.

"Please meet my boor of a partner, Richard Graves."

Her heart plummeted as she leveled her eyes on that menace, before turning her scowl on Rafael. "You shouldn't be walking around with him so blithely. Without a leash, too."

Rafael laughed. "I promise you I have him well in hand. Invite us in, *querida*."

"No."

Rafael's smile tried to coax her. "Not even now that he got what he deserves?" He shoved Graves forward.

Graves rolled his eyes, moved into the light of her foyer and showed her the right side of his face. It was a swollen deep purple beneath the beard he now sported. After he'd given her a good look, he stepped back, resettled that harsh gaze on her.

She blinked dazedly up at Rafael. "You hit him?"

"You think I'd do anything less once I found out what he'd done? What he'd said to you?"

She turned her gaze to Graves. "You told him about propositioning me, huh?"

"Of course."

Suddenly, a realization hit her, made her turn anxiously back to Rafael. "Is that how you hurt your hand?"

Rafael nodded. "You think anything less than his concrete jaw can break my bones?"

She gaped at him. "Your hand is really broken?"

"I do have fissures in two metacarpal bones."

She dragged him inside, heart squeezing as she feathered anxious touches over his splint. "God—and I made fun of your injury! I thought it was a sprain or something and you were only teasing me."

"No teasing." Graves walked in without invitation and closed the door behind him. "Under your thrall, he went and broke his hand. After I spent years teaching him how to fight without ever injuring himself. Terrible student." A mirthless laugh. "And he didn't even get his boo-boo kissed for his trouble."

She took Rafael down on the couch with her and glared up at Graves. "Oh, he will now. And then he'll get everything kissed. Anything that hasn't already been, that is."

At Graves's raised eyebrows, Rafael turned to him with a triumphant smile. "For the record, I didn't employ your generously imparted techniques because I just wanted to hurt you. And myself. I was the one who gave you the impression you can be rude to Eliana when I walked away from her."

"Is he always that vicious to women he thinks you're done with? Or is he that brutal by default? Which wouldn't surprise me. He doesn't feel quite human to me."

Graves turned his gaze to Rafael. "Very astute, this one. Foolishly outspoken, too. You may have to keep her."

Rafael's eyes ate her up. "Oh, I am keeping her."

She mock scowled at him. "How kind of you both. But I've been known to keep myself, thank you. So why don't you unstoppable forces of nature just run along and go exude charisma and testosterone all over someone else?"

Graves's lips spread. "It really looks like you'll have to keep her."

Rafael gave an exaggerated sigh. "If only *she* keeps *me*."

Graves tsked. "I trained you better than that, Numbers."

"Seems all your efforts went down the drain, Cobra."

She gaped at them. "Numbers? Cobra? You have code names in that brotherhood of yours?"

Graves raised one eyebrow at Rafael. Seemed he was surprised Rafael had told her about that. Not that Rafael had told her much. Rafael gave him a "deal with it" shrug.

"Numbers…" she mused. "I don't really see why you got named that. But Cobra is definitely apt. Though a more accurate name would be the raw material of deadliness. Like Venom."

This time Graves guffawed. "You're definitely keeping her."

Rafael's smile widened before it faded gradually. "Now, apologize to Eliana or I'll break my other hand and your jaw this time."

Ignoring him, Graves fixed his gaze on her, his British accent deepening. "He talks big, even when he knows he's in one piece because I have this inexplicable fondness for him. That said, and knowing that I'm doing this out of my deeply buried gentlemanly tendencies, I do apologize. If only for…"

She raised both hands. "Stop. Quit while you're ahead."

Rafael gathered her to him. "Is he forgiven?"

A harrumph. "On probation."

He chuckled and devoured her lips. She smiled against his lips at Graves's vocal disgust.

After Rafael released her reluctantly, she kissed his splint, then each finger. "No more breaking anything for me, okay?"

His head shake was adamant. "No promises."

Sighing her frustration at his terminal machismo, she looked between him and Graves. "At least no more fights between you two because of me, hear?"

Richard bowed in mock deference. "I'll do whatever it takes to keep your boy toy in optimum working condition."

And she laughed. That daunting dude had a sense of humor after all. She might even end up liking him.

Jumping up, she looked between the two men. "If you're good tycoons, I'll invite you to eat my magical seafood medley. You even get to help prepare it."

Rafael sprang to his feet. "I'm very, very good."

"I'm very, very nauseous" was Graves's contribution.

She and Rafael laughed, then headed to her kitchen. Muttering what sounded like paint-peeling expletives, Graves followed.

The evening turned out to be an unqualified success.

Eliana was the perfect hostess. She orchestrated all the details with ease and efficiency and handled them, men the world bowed to, with utmost confidence and grace. Richard miraculously kept his snark to a minimum, even followed her lead as she made them her sous-chefs while preparing the seafood medley, which did turn out to be magical.

Time flowed over and after dinner as they cleaned up then adjourned to her living room to drink hot *yerba maté,* eat *cocadas*—a traditional coconut confection—chat and verbally duel. Eliana held her own with Richard like no one he'd ever seen. Then, nestling into him on the couch, she started yawning.

Kissing her forehead, he gestured to Richard, who rose to his feet at once.

As he made to follow, she clung to him. "Stay."

His blood hurtled through his veins with temptation. "You need to sleep."

She rubbed her sleepy face into his neck, burning him wherever she touched. "I need to sleep with you."

"Tomorrow. I'll come alone."

She looked across at Richard. "You can go home on your own, right, Graves?"

"It's Rafael who can't. I have to tuck him in."

"Should have known you'd be no help." She clung to Rafael's neck. "At least carry me to bed."

"You, my enchantress, *are* wily."

"I just want you."

"And I want nothing but you." He kissed her pout as he rose and her arms fell off his shoulders like petals. "Lock up after us."

He rushed Richard out before he succumbed. They strode to the elevator with him already suffering withdrawal.

"What are you going to do with her?"

At Richard's quiet question, he exhaled. "None of your business, Cobra. Your role here is done."

Richard pressed the elevator button. "One piece of advice. A warning, really. This woman will turn you inside out."

"Don't you believe she already has?"

"I thought so. But now that I've been exposed to her, to this…live thing between you, I know I've been optimistic in my evaluation. This?" He made a gesture at all of him. "What you're feeling now? Is nothing to what you will feel a week from now. In a month's time, you'll be totally lost in her."

He cocked an eyebrow as they entered the elevator. "So you like her now?"

"I don't like anyone. But her? She's lethal."

He frowned. "You still think she's her father's accomplice? That her orphanage work has sinister motivations? You think I'd look the other way if I suspected such a thing?"

Richard shook his head. "I actually believe your verdict

of her benevolence. And that's what makes her deadly. She's for real. You'll have no defenses against her."

"Who says I want any?"

Richard fell silent as the elevator crowded with more and more people in this city that didn't sleep. Once out on the street, and before they went their separate ways, he said, "Are you giving up your revenge?"

His heart fisted. "I will never do that."

"Then do you have any idea how to have it and have her, too?"

"I'll figure out a way."

Richard only gave him a "sure you will" scowl before turning and walking away.

He watched Richard recede, his mind in an uproar.

He *would* destroy her father. He had to. But if she ever suspected he was the one who had done it, he could lose her. He couldn't even contemplate that.

This meant that his plan to let Ferreira know it was him who destroyed him was out of the question. He'd have to burn every bit of evidence leading back to him so she'd never know.

The one way this wouldn't be necessary was if in a month's time he cooled toward her. He could strike at her father and not fear the fallout to their relationship.

But he didn't need time to know it would only intensify, this all-consuming passion he felt for her.

And that was his verdict as the man who was never wrong.

They stumbled all the way from the mansion's doors to Rafael's master suite, snatching at each other with wrenching lips, straining against each other as if they'd merge.

It took a while to get there, as Rafael's suite spanned the whole fourth level. At least he'd made sure the mansion was empty before he got her here, after everyone who worked there had managed to walk in on them during the past three weeks.

He threw her down on his extra-large king-size bed and she slid over the satin sheets to its middle as he launched himself over her. She bowed up to intensify his impact, loving his weight and ferocity as he bore down on her.

His lips mashed against hers, his tongue plunging inside her while his hips rammed between her splayed thighs through their clothes.

He rose to snatch her top over her head, bunching her skirt to her waist then tearing her panties off her hips. As her legs fell wide apart for him, his hands, big enough to span her waist, raised her against the headboard. Then he buried his face in her confined breasts.

The sight of the dark majesty of his head against her made her keen, pressing his head harder to her aching flesh.

He muttered something deep and driven, the sound spearing her heart as his hands went to her back, releasing breasts now peaked and swollen for his ownership.

Imprisoning her hands above her head in his good one, he drew back to gaze at her. His eyes crackled with lust at how she must look. Like she had that first night, almost naked, the image of pure wanton abandon.

Growling, he let go of her hands to greedily take her breasts in his hands. She arched off the bed in the shock of pleasure, making a fuller offering of her flesh. He kneaded her, pinched her nipples, had her writhing…begging.

He tore his shirt off, exposing the body she'd told him made Greek gods seem like weaklings. Her awed hands shook over his burnished, sculpted perfection. His growls roughened as he rubbed his chest against her breasts until she thrashed.

"Querida…" He bent and opened his mouth fully over her breasts as if he'd devour her. Pleasure jackknifed through her with each hard draw of his lips, each hot swirl

of his tongue, until she was shuddering all over, her readiness flowing down her thighs.

She lay powerless under the avalanche of need as his hand glided over her, taking every liberty before settling between her thighs. His strong, sensitive fingers slid to her intimate flesh, now throbbing its demand for his touch. As his lips clamped hers, his fingers opened the lips of her femininity, slid between her folds, soaking in her arousal.

It took only a few strokes of those virtuoso fingers to spill her over the edge. She convulsed with pleasure, screeching it into his mouth.

His stroking fingers completed her pleasure, circling her nub soothingly. Desire seared through her again instead, that emptiness that gnawed her all the time now unbearable.

She drummed her feet against the bed in a fit of frustration. *"Just take me."*

He cupped her core, gathered her still trembling body to his, shushing her. And she knew he still wouldn't take her.

She turned her face into his chest, sobbed. "You once said you didn't want my heart pounding or me agitated. My heart is hammering, and I'm far beyond agitated...*all the time.*"

"You're just aroused."

She glared up at him. "Gee.,.I didn't realize that!"

His face was a mask of savage hunger even as he smiled at her. "I mean you're too aroused to think straight. Three weeks ago you didn't want to see me again."

"Three weeks ago I asked you to take me. Just like I've been doing every day ever since."

"You were trying to get rid of me then."

"Maybe I just couldn't wait to have you. Just like I can't now. Didn't you think of that?"

"I want us to have this first, *querida,* the courting, the anticipation, all the routes to pleasure but the ultimate one. When I join our bodies I want you certain that you want me inside you, not just the release I'll bring you."

Her fingers twisted in his hair, eyes pleading. "I *am* certain. I've been certain since the moment I saw you."

"But when you were thinking straight, you knew what was best for you, for us, wanted me to slow down."

"Not to *this* extent."

"You sound as if I've been tormenting you for months."

"It feels like *years*."

His smile devoured her brimming with pure male satisfaction. "I love you on fire for me like that."

She almost blurted out "I love *you*" but bit it back at the last moment.

She had no illusions about the nature of his involvement, didn't want her far different and more intense feelings to alarm him or put him off. There was no way a man like him would be hers except transiently. And she felt as if the more time that passed, the shorter the time she'd have him in full intimacy.

And now he was going away. He was traveling with one of his "brothers" to Japan. Even though he promised it would be only for a few days, it felt as if it would curtail her time with him further.

All troubled thoughts came to an end as he spread her thighs wide and slid down her trembling body.

Then he spoke against her molten feminine lips. "Let me ease the burning in your blood, *querida*."

He had been doing so in every way but the one she craved.

She tried to close her legs, needing him, not release. "What about the burn in your blood?"

"You can ease that if you wish."

"Oh, I wish, I so wish."

It was what ameliorated the gnawing, when he let her worship him. Getting intimate with the daunting beauty and massive proportions of him sent a frisson of danger through her as she wondered if it was possible he'd fit inside her.

But she couldn't wait until he did, yearned for the pain she knew he had to inflict. She wanted it to hurt at first, needed him to brand her with agony as his.

But though the intimacy gave him release, it only drove her madder with hunger, and left him harder and more on edge.

"Then you shall have your wish. Right after I have mine."

And he took her core in a hot, tongue-thrusting kiss and the world vanished in a whiteout of sensation....

"Can you please turn the anxious vibes down? They're drilling holes in the hull."

Rafael's head snapped up at the sarcastic tone. He watched its owner blankly as Raiden sat down in his private jet's plush seat, facing him.

As Raiden buckled his seat belt with a bedeviling look in his slanting eyes, Rafael's aggravation shot to maximum again.

"I would," he snarled, "if your damn pilot picked a route where I got cellular coverage."

Raiden aka Lightning had asked him to accompany him to Tokyo five days ago. He'd had the biggest lead yet in his quest to establish his bloodline and he needed him to examine records that couldn't be moved out of their institutes and temples and to come up with a pattern. He had. And Raiden had finally uncovered his legacy.

Rafael had only uncovered the meaning of agony.

Richard's prediction about time worsening his condition had come to pass. But then, hadn't it always been that bad? It was now a full month since he'd met Eliana, and he *was* fully submerged.

Since he'd left her side, he'd called her a dozen times per day. Given the opportunity, he would have had her on speakerphone all day. Would have had her on webcam all night.

Then came the torture of the twenty-four hour flights

from and back to Rio. For twelve of those, cellular transmission was cut. Being unable to call her for that long frayed his nerves. On the outbound flight, he'd managed to rein in his discomfort. Now, he was going ballistic.

Raiden had remained respectful of his agitation at first. But now he was outright making fun of his condition.

"My pilot says there should be transmission any time now." Raiden smoothed back the hair he'd cut short for the first time in his life, in preparation for entering the conservative upper crust of Japanese society. "But you still can't turn on your phone, since we're starting our descent."

Rafael hurled at him an infuriated glance. "Why are you talking when you don't have something useful to say?"

"Whoa, Numbers." Raiden grinned, stretching his long legs, the eyes he knew froze people in their tracks twinkling with mischief. "You were the last one, after Richard and Numair, that I thought I'd ever see in this state over a woman."

"And in this state, I'm liable to do things the Numbers you know wouldn't. So shut *up*, Lightning."

Raiden didn't shut up. Not until Rafael hurled state-of-the-art headphones at his thick skull. He outright guffawed then.

Caring nothing about their descent, Rafael had his phone out and turned on. Hands shaking with inexplicable and all-encompassing anxiety, he accessed his voice mail. There was one from Eliana.

Then the message began.

"Rafael…I—I've been in an accident…. They're taking me to Copa D'or Hospital. Oh, God…where are you?"

A loud clattering noise followed, as if she'd dropped the phone.

Then there was nothing more.

Eight

Rafael lost his mind.

With every heartbeat, he lost it again and again.

Eliana's phone was out of service. She wasn't in Copa D'Or, the hospital that was flooded with casualties in the aftermath of the accident.

A dump truck exceeding the allowed height had smashed into a pedestrian bridge, which had collapsed onto dozens of cars in the morning rush hour. Four people were killed. Dozens had injuries ranging from minor to critical. He turned the place upside down looking for her, questioned everyone. No one could report on Eliana's condition. Or where she'd gone.

Richard believed this meant she was well enough to walk out on her own. But the only thing that mattered to Rafael was that he couldn't reach her, couldn't protect her. His men and Richard's were combing the streets and had already looked in all the places she could be. She wasn't at her apartment or at her father's villa in Copacabana or his offices. Neither was her father, who Rafael belatedly remembered was back in San Francisco. And the damn man's phone was out of service, too.

Long past his wits' end, he charged over to the last place he could think of. His mansion.

Of her usual haunts, it was the farthest away from the hospital, more than a two-hour drive in this traffic. And there was no reason she should go there with him out of town and with her own apartment only twenty minutes away. But he had nowhere else to try.

Feeling the world crumbling around him, he arrived at his mansion just after dusk. The guards said no cars had come near the gates. And the mansion was empty since he'd given everyone time off while he was away.

He still tore through the mansion roaring for her. Then he exploded into his bedroom...and almost keeled over.

She was on his bed.

Curled on her side with her back to the door, her hair was a wild mass of loose curls rioting across his pillow. Her pastel green skirt suit was ripped in places and smudged in soot and blood.

And she wasn't moving.

Feeling like he had when he'd had too many brutal punches to the head, he staggered toward her, heartbeats shredding his arteries.

He crashed to his knees beside the bed, terror razing through him.

He couldn't touch her. He couldn't discover that she... she...

No. She was all right. She'd come all the way here. She must just be exhausted from the ordeal....

But she was so still. As if she wasn't breathing.

Throat sealing shut with panic, his tongue swelled, twisted on butchered pleas. "*Eu imploro, por favor, meu amor*...Eliana, I beg you please...wake up."

Nothing happened. No response. And he knew.

If she didn't wake up, he didn't want to live.

With the new certainty, knowing he wouldn't suffer long without her if she weren't with him anymore, he finally had the strength to reach out and touch her.

His shaking hand closed over her neck. And before a heartbeat could reanimate him, her heat devastated him.

Warm, hot, and she…she…

She opened her eyes.

"Rafael…"

That tremolo was a thousand volts to his heart, reanimating it after it had shriveled. And he was all over her, his hands everywhere, exposing her flesh, gliding over every inch, making sure all of her was intact, was functioning… was there.

A maddened beast rumbled in his gut at every bruise and graze he found. It dismantled his mind all over again that he'd been unable to prevent her injuries and was now unable to erase them. His lips documented each and every one, tried to soothe and seal them, pouring litanies of regret all over her for failing to do so.

All he could do was have her skin to skin, no barriers for the first time, exposing himself totally for her to take of his power, and for him to absorb her ordeal into himself.

As if he was succeeding, her enervated arms started to cling, her limp body to strain against him until he felt they'd merge. Then her feverish sobs started to make sense.

"My…my driver…was crushed. I—I tried to get him out…but I—I couldn't…then I was facedown on the ground and they were taking me away.… And I only thought of you…had to reach you…but got only your voice mail… then my phone died…"

His body convulsed around hers, holding her tight as weeping overpowered her, his lips drinking her tears, pledging over and over, "I'm here now. I'll never leave you again."

Her hacking sobs became words again. "I—I lost my purse, had only my phone…gave it to the taxi driver as fare. But he said coming all the way here would take him another hour out of his way in the opposite direction, so he dropped me on the main road…."

And he finally found something he could put right. "I'm going to find that driver, and I'm going to make him regret every contemptible act he's committed in his life."

Her tears suddenly stopped, her eyes widening with dismay. "No, no…it doesn't matter…."

"Don't try to stay my hand, Eliana. This sorry excuse for a man not only took your phone—your only method of communication—in lieu of fare, instead of getting you a charger, but then he left you stranded miles away from your destination, injured and alone. He *will* pay."

The next second he wanted to bludgeon himself at the way she seemed to shrivel at his aggression, even when it was on her behalf. She was so shaken, felt so fragile, as if she was…

Dread swept him all over again. What if she was hurt internally, something that would manifest gradually…?

"*Deus, meu amor*…I have to take you back to the hospital."

She resisted when he scooped her up. "There's nothing wrong with me."

"You can't know that. Some injuries, like concussions, become symptomatic later. You need to be monitored…."

"But nothing even came near me. The half of the car I was in was totally untouched."

"But the scratches and bruises all over you…?"

"I got those as I tried to get my driver out."

"But you said you found yourself facedown when they came to take you. You could have lost consciousness."

"It was just a reaction to the horrific sight of my driver's injuries, the flood of adrenaline as I tried to extricate him, then when…when he died right before my eyes."

Helplessness pummeled him again because he knew that he couldn't rewind those terrible moments, wipe away their memories.

But he could do something else. "Still, a couple of nights in hospital are a must."

"They aren't. Apart from my self-inflicted bruises, they gave me a clean bill of health. But even though I miraculously escaped without a scratch, I was just…distraught thinking how I could have died or worse." Her eyes welled as she clung to him. "I needed to be where I can feel you. Then I found a damaged part of the wall around the estate and entered through it, as the gate was too far and I just had to get to your bed…."

Groaning with raw, gut-wrenching emotion, he pressed her to his heart. "I'm here now, *preciosa*. I found you and I'm never letting you out of my sight again. I'll keep you safe from now on. *Always*."

"You can't stop fate." Before he could swear he would, she went on, hands trembling over his burning flesh. "When that bridge was collapsing and I thought I'd die, I had only one regret…that I was never with you completely."

The insupportable thought that her life could have been snuffed out in seconds, that he could have lost her, ravaged him again.

Then she sobbed. "You can't stop fate, Rafael, but you can have *now*. Let me have you now, all of you. Take all of me and show me how alive you are. Show me how alive I am, *meu amor*."

Meu amor. She'd called him my love.

And everything inside him snapped.

He bore down on her, felt her heart beat to the same insane rhythm beneath his, knew she couldn't bear preliminaries or gentleness, needed him to reaffirm her life ferociously.

Hand bunching in her locks, tethering her head down to the mattress, his eyes captured her streaming ones as he rose between her splayed thighs and pressed his crown to her molten entrance. Then he lunged.

He felt her flesh trying to ward off his invasion, tearing around his advance. Her shriek boomed inside his head as he pummeled through her barrier. Her body bowed beneath him, a deep arch of agony, but her nod was frantic. She wanted him to give her a ravishing, a full possession. He'd give her everything he had.

He withdrew through the clinging ring that clamped him like a vise, then thrust back harder, tore through the rest of her innocence, felt the scald of her blood and submission gush around him, coating his shaft.

Her cries became pain mixed with exultation, ripping through him. They became whimpers of loss as he withdrew until only the head of his erection remained caught in her flesh. Then he powered his unbearably hard length back into her mind-blowing tightness and heat, forging a new path inside her. His alone. His only home.

Bending, he sealed her lips with his, swallowed her gusting breaths and tortured keens as her flesh began to yield to his shaft, sucking him into an inferno of sensation.

The carnality, the reality, the *meaning* of being inside her... It was too much. He needed to give his all to her, to lose himself inside her, to pierce her essence and consume her.

He glided out of her tightness, pummeled back just as she pumped up, impaling herself further on his erection. Pleasure detonated, almost blew out his arteries.

"Eliana—there can't be pleasure like this, there can't be. Take it all, Eliana, give it all to me...."

"Yes...Rafael...*yes*."

She crushed herself against him, catapulting him into a frenzy. He pounded into her now, building in force and cadence, had her voluptuous breasts jiggling beneath him, her trembling legs spreading wider as her core poured more welcome over him.

The heat, the friction escalated until he sensed the heart thundering beneath his might burst with need for release.

Tilting her hips, he angled himself, still unable to sink inside her to the root through the tightness of her untried body. But he adjusted his position, seeking her inner triggers to ignite her release. Until he did.

Shrieking, she shattered around him, her flesh wringing his shaft with convulsions, the flood of her release razing him, its current snapping his sanity.

He detonated inside her, streams of ecstasy scalding through his length, pouring into her womb, his seed mixing with her pleasure in jet after jet of pure culmination.

Everything started to vanish. Only Eliana remained, her being and flesh melting into his....

Rafael came to with a gasp.

As his senses flickered back, he realized he'd lost consciousness...for the first time in his life. The discharge of fright and craving had been that brutal. It hadn't been a sudden blackout, but a descent into a realm where he'd merged with Eliana on every fundamental level there was.

He lifted his weight from her cushioning softness on shaking arms. She came to only when he moved, her core involuntarily clutching the hardness that hadn't subsided a bit, dragging a groan of pleasure from his depths.

Her eyes fluttered open and he saw how red and puffy they were, and the memory of her ordeal twisted his gut.

But when her lips spread into such a smile, as if she'd discovered an exclusive secret, her eyes growing heavy with such fulfillment, it made him feel like thumping his chest.

The next second, the bite of shame at the ferocity with which he'd initiated her doused his self-satisfaction.

She whimpered as he began to pull out. "Stay inside me."

He stilled. "You must be sore."

"Oh, I am…magnificently so." Her silky legs caressed his sides, her heels digging into his buttocks, driving him back inside her. "If I knew just how incredible it would be to be ravished by you, I would have found a way to make you do it to me before. As it was, it took a near-fatal accident to break your resolve." Her eyes darkened before she made an effort to brighten them. "Being an overachiever in everything, you went and knocked me out with too much pleasure."

Heart quivering with the enormity of everything that had happened in the past several hours, he said, "You knocked me out, too, and I don't even have your excuse of being a novice."

Her eyes widened. "I did?"

"Indeed. I blinked out for the very first time in my life. I never have, even when I got punched square in the face. Richard used to say I have something in my head that doesn't cut out. It took you to KO me."

Her look of delight and smugness was worthy of a hundred portraits. It had a chuckle bursting on his lips as his heart expanded with gratitude. That she existed, was whole, and was his—in every way now.

Debilitated with relief, he rolled onto his back, taking her with him, staying inside her as she'd demanded. She enveloped him in intimacy, her hair gleaming waves of silk strewn over his chest.

He traced the exquisite profile pressed over his heart, the velvet limbs entangled with his. Dismay surged again at her bruises, at how much worse it could have been.

He exhaled the excess fright, the mounting guilt. "And to think I once asked if you were a virgin so I'd adjust my approach. Then I realize you are one and I still take your virginity with all the finesse of a plundering marauder."

She raised his head, eyes urgent. "I needed you, too. I couldn't bear any more gentleness. I needed you to take me with all your strength, to give me the full ferocity of your life and mine, no holds barred. The pain only made the pleasure almost too much to bear. I think I did die for a while with it."

His arms convulsed around her. "You will always *live* with it. Live and thrive and be your vivacious, bursting-with-life delight of a self, do you understand?"

She nodded, eyes growing dreamy. "And I want to live every possible second with you inside me."

"The hard part for me would be *not* being inside you." He thrust deeper inside her hot tightness.

Throwing her head back with a cry, her eyes filled again.

As he cursed himself and tried to withdraw from her depths, she tightened her inner grip on him, her heat and tightness becoming unbearable.

"I need you again, Rafael."

"It would hurt more, with you already so sore."

"I want it to hurt."

Holding her now-feverish eyes, he read her need. He'd always do whatever it took to fulfill each and every one.

Sweeping her to her back, he spread her beneath him and lay down on top of her. She needed more proof that she'd survived, and only something as intense as pain-mixed plea-sure could make her feel truly alive now.

She writhed beneath him, her desire flowing, arousal blazing in her eyes. She needed him to ride her and domi-nate her and wring her of every spark of sensation. Make her live to the fullest.

As he started moving inside her again, trying to work up the heart to give her the ferocity she needed, knowing it would hurt her, the belated realization dawned on him.

He'd taken her without protection. He was doing so again.

But there was no thought of consequences. In fact, he

welcomed them. He wanted—*needed*—her pregnant with his child.

This woman he loved with everything in him. This woman he'd die for; he'd no longer wanted to live when he'd thought he'd lost her. He wanted her bound to him by every shackle.

He already had those of desire and ecstasy. But now he had to make sure he had the most binding ones of all. Love. And a child.

That would be how he'd brand her as his forever, in every way, so when he finally struck her father down, and if she ever found out, he wouldn't lose her.

Ellie spread her legs wider for Rafael, her nails sinking into his back and buttocks, urging him on. It hurt having him inside her, but she felt she'd implode if he withdrew. She needed his flesh filling her this way, to hold her together.

Her whole being was still in shock. Revolting at the horrors she'd witnessed, petrified at the brush with death.

When he hadn't answered her, she'd lost her mind. The need for any part of him had been what had driven her. She would have walked here just to be where his feel and scent were.

Then he was here and enveloping her in his passion and protection and the world righted itself. It was frightening how dependent she was on him, but it was also exhilarating. To know that he existed, the only one to make her truly alive.

Now anything she'd *thought* she'd known about intimacy had been decimated. From the moment he'd invaded her, joined their bodies, taken her to the very limits of her mortality. It had been beyond description, transfiguring. She was now a totally different person. A woman. *His woman.* At last.

Aware of what pleasure was now—profound, pervasive,

overpowering pleasure, she was maddened for more. For the proof of his life and hers. The pain only intensified their union, confirmed his absolute domination and her utter surrender.

Rafael now loomed above her, the struggle to control his power blazing on his face. He withdrew, then in one burning plunge pierced her to her recesses.

The shock to her system was total.

Paralyzed with too much sensation, she stared up at him. This sublime suffering *was* more intense than the first time. The scream that ripped from her throat was the sum total of her every cell shrieking with life.

He rested within her, stretching her beyond capacity, seemingly as incapacitated as she was at her captivation. Pride played on her lips as blackness frothed from the periphery of her vision, a storm front of pleasure advancing from her core.

It was he who broke the panting silence, his voice feral. "Eliana, the pleasure of you…*Deus*…"

He rose on his palms, withdrawing again, dragging a shriek of loss from her. She clung blindly, crazed for his branding pain and pleasure. He gave them to her, driving back inside her.

On his next withdrawal, she lost what was left of her mind. She thrust her hips up, seeking his impalement. He bunched her hair in his fist, tugged her down to the bed, exposing her throat, latching his teeth into her flesh.

"Yes, Rafael," she cried out. "Eat me up…finish me."

"I will. I always will."

He plowed back into her, showed her that the first time he'd taken her, her inexperienced flesh had impeded his advance. This time, those first plunges had just been preparations. Now he fed her core more with every pounding thrust, causing an unbelievable, almost unbearable expansion within her, until she felt him hit the epicenter of her very essence and unleashed everything inside her.

Ecstasy rent her with its intensity, had her shrieking, convulsing, clinging to him in her tumult. All through, her swimming vision clung to his magnificent face as he focused on completing her release until she saw it seize, tension shooting up in his eyes, as if unsure when to let go.

And she begged for him, for everything. "Give me— give me…"

And he gave. She felt each throb and surge of his climax inside her. The hot jets hit her intimate, swollen flesh, had her thrashing, weeping, unable to endure the spikes in pleasure as everything dimmed, faded….

Awareness trickled between cottony layers of fulfillment. Then Ellie realized what had roused her. Rafael was rising off her, leaving her body.

Before she could whimper with his loss, she moaned her contentment. More bliss settled into her bones as he swept her around, draped her over his expansive body, stayed inside her, mingling their sweat and satisfaction.

Closing her eyes, she let the moment integrate into her cells. She'd need these precious memories to tide her over for the rest of her life.

When one day this ended.

But it wasn't over yet. And she'd cherish every moment with him. Celebrate being alive and desired by him for any length of time.

"If I'd known how it would be between us…" his voice rumbled beneath her ear. "That it would far exceed even my perfectionist fantasies, I *would* have taken you weeks ago."

She raised a wobbling head, marveled anew at his beauty, and at how incredible their bodies looked entwined.

"See? Next time just give in to my demands."

His lips curved. "I certainly will. But then I think we

needed this past month, of deepening our knowledge and appreciation of each other and suffering denial, to reach this unprecedented level of intimacy and ecstasy."

"If you say so."

"I do." He tugged her hair, turning her face to where he was pointing. "See this?"

"Your jacket?"

"Yes. The jacket full of protection I didn't use."

She rose on trembling arms, palms on his sculpted chest, dismay surging. She hadn't even thought of protection. Again.

Or had she...?

In a heartbeat, she saw a whole realm of possibility, a life revolving around a baby with raven hair and silver eyes.

She sat up, feeling his seed inside her, transforming her from girl to woman, a woman who'd give anything for it to take root in her womb.

But that was her. He wouldn't feel the same.

"You could be already pregnant."

She looked away. "You don't need to worry about it."

His finger beneath her chin turned her face back to his, but she kept her eyes averted. She didn't want to see anxiety in his eyes, and the beginning of the end.

"Look at me, *meu coração.*"

The way he said that—*my heart*—dragged her eyes back to his. And what she saw in them had now-familiar hot tears crowding behind hers.

"Though I hope you're not, just because I would like us to have more time to ourselves before we become parents— there's nothing I want more than for you to eventually carry my child."

Her throat closed, emotions a burning coal. "Rafael..."

"*Eu te amo,* Eliana, my answer to my every prayer."

She stared at him. Had he really said *I love you?*

"I believe I loved you at first sight, and even before that. I believe I've been waiting for you my whole life, recognized you even before I saw you. Now I know I can't live without you. Literally." He sighed deeply. "Today, when I thought I might lose you, I no longer wanted to live. I want you with me forever, *meu amor*. And I want our forever to start now." A touch that was worship itself cupped her trembling face. "Tell me you want me forever, too. Tell me you love me."

She tried to obey his command, blurt out all that was in her heart. But she couldn't breathe. His words, his confessions… As usual, he was too much.

"You don't love me?" He rose beneath her, scowling. Then a look of absolute arrogance gripped his face. "You might not love me yet, but you will. I will make you love me."

That made her splutter, "Are you kidding? Wasn't it the most blatant thing in existence that I loved you from the first moment, too?" She cupped his face, hands trembling in wonder. "I love you so much it's been a constant pain and dread."

His frown was back full scale. "Why pain and dread?"

"Because I thought you'd never feel the same. Because I thought you'd one day walk away and I'd never see you again."

His scowl deepened. "How could you think such non-sense? Haven't I been showing you in every minute and in every way how much I feel for you? And I'm never, ever, walking away."

Knowing it would take her a while, maybe forever, to come to terms with the idea that he felt all that for her, she exhaled raggedly. "Now I have one regret."

"I can't have you feeling any such thing."

"Oh, it's a benign one. I now wish I didn't tell you I love you totally. I would have loved to see what lengths you'd go to 'to make me love you.'"

"No need to wonder or imagine. I will go to all those lengths anyway. To that end, I'll need to make you my wife."

She gaped at him.

He dragged her to him, possessed her lips in a kiss that almost extracted her soul before he withdrew, his voice a deep, ragged entreaty. "Marry me, Eliana."

Nine

Ellie bent to taste the powerful pulse in Rafael's neck.

Dragging her teeth down his shoulder and chest, she whispered hot, explicit words of desire into his flesh.

Then she came to the scar that was the one thing marring his perfection. It snaked from his back over his left kidney around to his abdomen below his ribs. He'd only told her it was an emergency surgery when he was much younger, and wouldn't go into specifics. It hurt her, terribly, every time she saw it or touched it. But it didn't seem to hurt him. And when she touched it, like now, especially with her lips and tongue, it sent him berserk. As she traced it now with both, his great body shuddered beneath her on a long groan of torment.

Feeling all-powerful eliciting such desire from him, she squeezed his steel buttocks as she slid her leg between his muscled, hair-roughened ones, her knee pressing an erection that felt harder and more daunting than ever before.

It never ceased to amaze her, the constantly renewable

need they shared. They were both on fire again and it had been only an hour since they'd last made love.

Like always with him, time warped. It had been six weeks already since he'd asked her to marry him. Since she'd said an inordinate number of yeses. And those six weeks felt at once like six hours and six years. So much had happened since. So many experiences, so much delight. So much love.

Love. She still couldn't believe it sometimes. Rafael loved her. As much as she loved him. Though being the supreme alpha male who had to be superior in everything, he insisted he loved her more. *Way* more, according to him. She'd only said she had a lifetime to prove him wrong on that front.

She'd moved in with him that same day. Or rather, she'd stayed where she was. He'd assigned her a PA who'd gone to her place to pack everything in meticulously sorted boxes and to get her out of her lease. He wasn't about to let her keep a place a two-hour drive away, and if he had his way, she wouldn't drive again. Or be in a car again. He actually assigned her a helicopter to take her to and from her father's offices.

She let him shower her with extravagances. For now. He was too rattled by her accident and was overreacting. She would gradually pull him back from the extremes he now went to—to protect and pamper her—to a more rational level.

Though in one arena, she really hoped he'd never stop being excessive. In bed. Those unusual demands he'd said he'd make on her that first night? That had been an understatement.

If anyone had told her in her oblivious inexperience that she'd meet the insatiable demands of a sex god like Rafael, she would have scoffed. What they had together shouldn't even be possible. But it was better than possible. It was real. And it was beyond description.

What made their intimacies even more incendiary was that they continued to be just as incredible together out of bed. Rafael was getting more and more embroiled in her work with her father, as well as her work at the orphanage. And he was letting her into his world, introducing her to his "brothers" and involving her in his work.

And that was where she'd discovered the level of his sheer, mind-boggling *genius.*

She now realized that his Numbers pseudonym was apt. He was a literal genius in that regard—and the ramifications of his ability were almost endless. Not that he appreciated it when she used that classification. He'd made it clear she shouldn't repeat it to *anyone,* because he never wanted anyone to know the true extent of his capabilities. It was very helpful for him to be underestimated.

Realizing "anyone" included her father, she made it clear that anything about him, or between them, would never be divulged to anyone else.

It remained the only dim area in the glittering wonderland that was her life with Rafael. That the man she loved was taking longer than expected to warm up to his future father-in-law. And that was when her father, seeing how magnificent Rafael was to her, now thought him an answer to his prayers, too.

Not that Rafael did anything to indicate he disliked her father. It was just…a feeling. Overtly, he went to every length to be attentive and welcoming, and he was taking serious interest in her father's business woes. He even had her providing him with all the details so he could come up with solutions. She had no doubt he would. After all, he *could* do anything.

Another thing she was gladly letting him orchestrate was their wedding.

She still could barely believe that in two weeks' time, she'd be Senhora Moreno Salazar. Or, as she'd told him while laughing until she cried, she'd be Eliana Larsen Ferreira Moreno Salazar.

Rafael had put the world at her disposal in preparing their wedding. But she'd insisted he do it instead, on the caveat that he made it a *very* simple ceremony. Just them, her father and half brothers and his brothers, right here on the mansion grounds.

She wasn't widening the circle to friends and colleagues because it would only detract from the real purpose of the ceremony. Their union. All she wanted was his ring on her finger, and to profess their vows in front of their nearest and dearest before rushing off to resume "plunging deeper into passion."

Yeah, that had turned out to be the only accurate way to describe what they had.

She now couldn't wait to tumble into that abyss once more.

Painting his body with her fingertips, trailing patterns over him with her hair, she chuckled when his whole body vibrated.

"I hope you know what you're inviting with this act of extreme provocation."

"Which act are you referring to?" She nipped his nipples, pouring fuel on his reignited passion, her own raging.

And it was his fault. In their last hour-long lovemaking session, he'd upgraded her experience from multiple to continuous orgasms. He'd sure created a monster. At least, a bigger monster than the one he had spawned from the start.

He grabbed her around the waist, lifting her as if her one hundred and forty pounds were minus the hundred, making her straddle him, scorching lust flaring in his eyes. "I have a list. Each with a consequence all its own."

She rocked against him, sliding the lips of her core up and

down his incredible length and girth and hardness, bathing him in her flowing arousal and their combined pleasure.

"Terrible consequences, I hope."

"Unspeakable." He dragged her down at the same moment he thrust upward, impaling her to her core.

Eyes rolling back, his name tore out of her, body and mind unraveling at the excruciating expansion and pleasure.

Then he was showing her the consequences of teasing him, his full force behind every ram, sparking orgasms from the trigger he hit over and over in her depths until all existence converged on him and what he was doing to her.

It soon became too much, and she shrieked for that final explosion that would finish her. As always, knowing just when to give it to her, he quickened his thrusts to a jackhammering rhythm until her body gushed molten agony. Just as ecstasy became a constant current, he roared and lodged into her womb, jetting his seed, filling her to overflowing.

She jerked with every hot wave of pleasure, her insides quivering, overloading—then blackness....

Reluctant to exit that realm of bliss but eager to rejoin Rafael, Ellie's eyelids drifted open. Slowly adjusting to the light, she saw he was now at the end of his expansive bedroom, theirs now, putting the last touches on his immaculateness in front of the full-length gilded mirror.

He met her gaze in the mirror at once, his nostrils flaring with that all-out passion she'd become addicted to and that now formed the foundation of her world.

"I didn't want to wake you. You looked so peaceful. All I wanted, of course, was to disrupt that peace and corrupt that apparent innocence, but regretfully, I have an appointment."

She kicked off the duvet he'd covered her with, stretching luxuriously, jutting her delightfully sore breasts at him. "One that couldn't be postponed for a mere half hour?"

"Temptress. I'll take it all out on you when I come back."

He strode back to her in all black, looking every inch the ruthless, unstoppable god of finance. "But for now, I'll have one for the road." Sitting down beside her, he pulled her into his arms, lips soothing her nipples, hands caressing her all over until she twisted in his arms, her breath hitching.

"Shh, let me take care of you, *meu alma*."

Her thighs fell apart for him, and his fingers sought her core knowingly, tenderly, as they plunged inside. Pumping into her while his thumb ground her bud in circles, in the exact pressure and speed to spill her into a hot, sharp climax almost at once.

Melting in his embrace, she sighed. "Even when pressed for time, my fiancé knows how to give me a sample of delights to come, to ensure he leaves me burning for more."

"It *is* my evil plan." Suddenly his lust-hooded gaze turned serious. "Speaking of plans...I wanted to talk to you about something."

She struggled to sit up, feeling this was big. "What is it?"

"It's about Diego, and the bond we share. I want to offer him more than visits and sponsoring. I want to discuss the possibility of fostering him or even adopting him. I know he's a little old to be your son, but maybe a younger brother..."

She leaped into his arms, clinging around his neck frantically. "*Yes*. Oh, God, yes, Rafael. Whatever you wish, whatever works. Diego is an angel and he loves you so completely. Oh, God, *I* love you so completely it *hurts*."

His eyes and lips filled with such tenderness. "As long as the hurt is a good one."

Burying her lips in his neck, she trembled with emotion. "The absolute best."

Pulling back, he caressed her flushed cheek. "I shouldn't have broached this huge subject when I have to run. But mull it over. Think practicalities and logistics. I realize it's a lot to take on, but I want us to do it. For Diego, and for us."

She nodded, a galaxy full of stars in her eyes as he kissed her and stood to leave.

Cupping her cheek, he pledged, "*Eu te amo, minha* Eliana, my answered prayers. The prayers I never even prayed."

She went back to sleep as soon as Rafael left, dreaming such wonderful dreams. All vague and unconnected to their reality or the new possibilities with Diego. But she woke up soaring. And almost certain about something.

An hour later, after calling one of those pharmacies that delivered, the "almost" part was gone.

She *was* pregnant.

Sitting down, heart pounding, she held the strip with the vivid pink lines in her hand.

This was…too much. Everything was too perfect. Too incredible. Rafael on his own was already all that. But his love, a future with him, with Diego joining their family… and now a baby already?

She was certain she'd conceived that first time he'd taken her. He'd claimed her so completely, and she'd surrendered so totally that night, needing him to put his mark on her. And he had. His seed had taken root inside her and was growing into a precious, little miracle.

She couldn't wait to tell him. Though he might be a bit disappointed he'd have to compete with his child so soon for her love and attention, it was up to her to show him he never had to worry. Her love for their baby would never interfere with hers for him. Never.

Jumping up, she dressed in a hurry, intending to surprise him. As he now no longer went to his offices on weekends, he was having his meeting in a hotel nearby. He never brought work and work-related people home. The only ones exempt from being considered work were his brothers.

Stopping, she groaned. She'd *forgotten*. He'd invited three of those intimidating Black Castle men for dinner.

After meeting the other two who were coming tonight, Raiden Kuroshiro and Numair Al Aswad, she considered Graves the lesser evil.

Rushing downstairs, she called Rafael's driver, and Daniel told her Rafael had finished his meeting and was already back home.

Joy swept her as she rushed to find him. It was 6:00 p.m. and his brothers should arrive around eight. She had time to tell him the news. And maybe for one more lovemaking session.

Approaching his study—"their place"—she heard him talking. Slowing down, she debated whether to walk in or wait until he finished his call. Then she heard another voice. Then another. His brothers were already here.

Dammit. What were they doing here so early?

As she stood undecided about what to do, one of them said something. It was Numair. She'd recognize his arctic voice anywhere. And what he'd said hit her between the eyes like an icicle.

He'd said, "We put our bigger plans on hold so you could come to Brazil and get close to Ferreira. We did only because you wanted the satisfaction of looking him in the eye as you destroyed him."

Before she could muster an explanation for those words, Rafael spoke and ended her fumbling efforts.

"Destroying him anonymously will do, as well."

"Stick with your original plan, Numbers." That was Raiden. Deceptively suave and even more deadly for it. "Once that guy is rotting in prison, you can walk up to him and tell him it was you who put him there. He wouldn't be able to do anything about it or say anything to anyone."

"Actually, your original plan is nothing compared to your new one," Numair said. "Landing his daughter, making her spill his secrets, is your best weapon yet. Right after the wedding, you can use it to strike him down and be done with it."

"Then you can tell him," Raiden added. "With his daughter in your bed and at your mercy, he'd keep silent forever."

Graves cracked a harsh laugh. "You, my boys, have no idea what kind of land mine you've just tripped over here."

Their voices kept coming closer. It was only when she found herself on the threshold of the room where her life had once changed forever that she realized she'd walked in on them.

They all rose as one. Dismay was the one thing she saw in their eyes. Something made her seek Rafael's last. Dread that she'd find confirmation in them. And that was exactly what she found.

"You want to destroy my father?" The voice that croaked out of her didn't sound like hers anymore. "You 'landed' me to bring down my father? That's why you've been milking me for information? Why you're marrying me?"

"Eliana, no…" He stopped, swung toward the others. "What are you waiting for? Get the hell out."

Raiden and Numair looked at him as if he'd gone mad. Then, with no trace of their earlier dismay, they regarded her stonily as they passed her on their way out. It was only Graves who looked almost as apologetic as he did.

Once alone, Rafael neared with the caution he'd use to approach a frightened gazelle. "I'm sorry you heard that."

Numbness spread. "That's all you have to say?"

His lips thinned, his jaw hardened more. "I would have given anything for you to never know that. Especially now."

"*Now?* That's your only problem? That I heard it before your plans come to fruition? That's the only reason you're upset? Because now that I've heard them, they won't?"

"I didn't want to upset *you.*"

"You want to send my father to prison, but you don't want to upset me?"

His eyes, the eyes of the man she'd loved with every fiber of her being till minutes ago, sparked with danger. "Your father deserves whatever I will do to him. But I wanted to spare you as much as I could."

And it registered at last. The blow of realization. What rewrote the past ten weeks, explained them far better than what had seemed too good to be true. Because it was.

This was the truth.

The ice that encased her started cracking. "Everything we've had…from the first moment…it was all a plot. A lie."

"No." He hauled her to him. "That first night was all true. I didn't realize who you were until I saw you with him."

She tore out of his embrace. Unable to go far, she slumped to the ground by the couch where they'd shared their first intimacy.

Swearing harshly, Rafael swooped over her, swept her up into his arms and sat down on the couch with her on his lap. Unable to push away again, she lay limply against him, tremors racking her body.

"That's why you walked away," she choked. "Then you realized you could use me…and came back as soon as you had another plan in place. Everything ever since…a lie. *Everything.*"

His arms convulsed around her. "No, Eliana. Everything between us was real. *Is* real."

Her head rolled weakly over his shoulder, her eyes refusing to meet his, tears beginning to fall. "I can see it all now. Everything that didn't register at the time. I always sensed something in you—a calculation—but I couldn't find any reason you'd be playing me. I would have never been paranoid enough to imagine it was never me you wanted, but just a weapon to use against my father."

"It was *always* you I wanted." Gripping her head, he tried to make her look at him. She finally did and tears flowed thicker. He looked exactly like the man she loved. That man who didn't exist. "I *never* intended to use you against him. And the only calculation you felt targeted your father."

"Now it all makes sense. The...viciousness I felt from you toward him. And I kept rationalizing it so I could be with you. And I ended up giving you everything you needed... to destroy my father." The first sob tore out of her. "All an act..."

He squeezed her tighter. "I *never* acted with you."

"I don't believe...anything you say...anymore."

"You have to. *Eu te amo,* Eliana—I love you and that's the only truth. And when you remember everything we had..."

"I do...remember." Her every word now got hacked in two, the pain unbearable. "Every touch...and word...and look. And they're all tainted with...what I now know."

His hands roamed her face and body, as if he'd wipe away what she now knew. "That's shock talking. You're just angry."

Sobs caught in her lungs, almost tore them apart. "I'm not...angry...I'm...destroyed. You...destroyed *me*...Rafael."

"No... *Deus,* Eliana, don't say that. I would never hurt you. I only care about you, about us."

"There is...no...us."

"There is nothing *but* us. My plans for your father have nothing to do with us. *Nothing.* And after our wedding..."

It finally hurt enough. It made her lurch out of his arms, tumble onto the couch, pushing against him as if he burned her. "You...think I'll go ahead with the wedding...as if nothing happened? As if you're still the man I loved?"

He burst to his feet, his frustration pummeling her. "If this had happened a month after the wedding, I would have already secured you, us."

This made tears and sobs stop abruptly. "If we'd been married ten years, it would have still ended things between us."

Stabbing his fingers through his hair, he exhaled heavily.

"I can see I'm not talking you down but just making it all worse. But I swear to you, Eliana, we have nothing to do with anything I ever planned for your father. I never lied to you about my feelings, and I never wanted to hurt you."

"Then prove it. Don't hurt *him*."

The fire went out in his eyes, that terrible, terrifying ice impaling her. "Your father has to pay."

And she wailed, *"Pay for what?"*

His face became an opaque mask. "It's nothing to do with us, Eliana. Nothing to do with you."

"It has *everything* to do with me. He's the most important person in my world."

His eyes flared again. "I thought that was me."

"I don't even know *who you* are anymore. But I know who he is. He's the man who's been there for me every single hour since I was born. He's my *father*."

She pulled at her finger in a frenzy, almost pulling it out of its socket. By the time she yanked his ring off, she was panting, weeping, shaking all over.

"Put my ring back on your finger, Eliana. *Now*."

Holding his volcanic gaze, she let the ring drop to the pristinely polished hardwood floor.

For one last moment, she looked up at him—the most incredible dream of her life, who'd turned out to be its most devastating nightmare. And said goodbye.

"If you're my father's enemy, you're my enemy, too."

Staggering around, she stumbled out of the room. Out of his mansion. Out of his life.

Where she'd never truly been.

Ten

Crumpled on a bed in some hotel, Ellie lay like something broken and discarded, the storm of misery buffeting her.

She hadn't been exaggerating when she'd told Rafael he'd destroyed her. He'd crushed something inside her. Her belief in her judgment, which balanced her, which she depended on to guide her through life. He'd done so once before only to heal it, then boost it to no end. Now he'd crushed it again, irrevocably this time, along with everything beautiful and hopeful inside her.

Just hours ago she'd been on top of the world, secure in the love of the man she adored, pregnant with his baby, and a couple of weeks away from marrying him. Now everything lay in ruins at the bottom of the hollow shell she'd become.

Everything had been a lie.

But how had she ever believed it had been real? The more she thought back, the more she remembered how he'd made her give him every detail of her father's work, the clearer it became that she'd always been a means to an end to him.

And *this* made sense. That she'd been just an instrument to him. How had she ever believed a man like him could love her like she loved him? Hadn't she already known that he was too much for her?

Then the avalanche began again.

Every second from the moment she'd laid eyes on him, every memory, so brutal in clarity, so heartrending in beauty, blasted holes in her heart. The cascade strengthened with every snippet of remembrance, decimating her self-worth, submerging her in humiliation. Every word she'd uttered, admiring and believing in him; every glance that hungered for him and adored him; every liberty she'd begged him to take with her body, with her being; every surrender and trust she'd bestowed on him, certain he'd treasure it.

The damage would only spread, deepen, until there was nothing left of her but ashes. And it had all been for nothing. She'd been nothing to him. Worse than nothing. She'd been the knife he'd been honing to stab her father with.

She could only be thankful he'd broken that knife before he had a chance to use it.

Suddenly, she bolted upright before slumping back, faint with the hours of soul-tearing weeping…and with true terror.

For her father.

Rafael was too powerful, could be—*was*—ruthless. Whether he wielded her as a weapon or not, there was no stopping him.

If only she could find out the reason for Rafael's enmity, she might find a way out. But she'd seen it in his eyes. He was never telling her why.

There was only one other possible source of info.

"Are you sure it's only a stomach bug?"

That was the fifth time her father had asked her that question inside five minutes. That had been the one thing she could think of to explain how horrible she looked.

Ellie nodded. "The worst of it is over."

Her reassurance did nothing to allay his anxiety. After her mother had complained of what they'd thought digestive troubles, which had turned out to be terminal cancer, her father had been a full-blown, worst-case-scenario worrywart. All her life, he'd been obsessed with her health.

"Daddy, please answer me."

She'd asked if he'd ever committed any serious indiscretion. He'd thought she was asking because she didn't believe untimely decisions were the only reason for the trouble his business was in. He really had no clue Rafael was after him or why he would be. At least this reassured her she wouldn't discover she didn't know her father, either.

Her father sagged down beside her on the couch, his unseeing eyes scanning the expansive living room, which was furnished in warm earth colors and had perfect panoramic views of the Atlantic.

He'd given this villa to her mother as a wedding present. She'd been the one to decorate it, and he hadn't changed a thing since. He'd been loath to come back for years after her death. Now it seemed it was where he found his only comfort.

"I'm sorry I never worked up the nerve to tell you, Ellie. I didn't want to lose your respect."

Heart pounding painfully, she squeezed his hand. "I'll never love you any less, Daddy. Just tell me."

A ragged exhalation. "After those losses hit me hard, I did some tax evasion to compensate, and everything got twisted out of all proportions. Now it's gone from bad to worse and I might declare bankruptcy soon." He dropped his head in his palms. "Oh, my little darling, I'm so sorry, but I have to confess something else. I was actually feeling desperate enough to ask Rafael for help. I know you don't want to ever mix your marriage with business, but I was thinking it would be child's play for Rafael to solve all my problems."

While tax evasion was bad, it didn't warrant Rafael's cold-blooded plan of revenge. She didn't believe her father *could* do anything to warrant it. But this was clearly a dead end.

Rising to her feet, she bent to kiss him. "Next time, promise you'll tell me everything so I can help before things snowball into a huge mess, okay?"

After her father promised, and she reassured him that they'd see this through, he saw her to the door, totally oblivious to the danger he was in and the devastation in Ellie's life.

Back at the hotel, she fell into bed, her mind churning as exhaustion dragged her under into tumultuous darkness.

She had to seek Rafael again. It was all in his hands. Everything was.

Her world, her being…her destruction.

Rafael. Always Rafael…

Warm power rejuvenated her drained body; delicious fire roamed her aching flesh. Sighing softly, she drove deeper into the solace, a moan of longing on her lips.

"Rafael…"

"*Si, meu amor, si*…I'm here, I'm yours."

The pledge felt like a resurrection, after the death her spirit had suffered.

Her eyes fluttered open. The phantasm had Rafael's face, his body, his hunger…and it—he…

He was really here!

Suddenly drowning, her body violently lurched against his, as if kicking up to a surface that didn't exit.

"Don't push me away, *meu alma*…"

And they overtook her, every agony and bitterness and

desperation, burning from her depths and gushing from her lips on racking, uncontrollable heaves.

Lost in the tumult, she felt Rafael carrying her to the bathroom, securing her in his infinite strength as the misery overpowered her. He held her, kissing and soothing her. Finally collapsing against him, empty and depleted, he stretched her in his arms on the floor, kneading the muscles that had almost torn with the violence of her retching. Then ridding her of her soiled clothes, stripping himself, he took her into the shower.

He held her up beneath the warm cascade, caressing and coddling her with such gentleness and patience. At last, he took her down on the floor of the shower, and the potency that had planted the miraculous seed of life inside scorched a furrow in her buttocks. He made no sensual overtures, his touch bolstering, not arousing, his body pressed to hers only to transfer his vitality into her. Yet the unwilling bliss she felt at his ministrations caught fire. Her insides cramped, clamoring for his occupation.

As always, in tune with the slightest nuance of her needs, he adjusted her position over his lap, pressing the wide crown of his erection against her opening. Her body melted, inside and out, her thighs splayed wider in submission.

Holding her eyes, hunger and entreaty and determination mingled in his. Reading her capitulation, he flattened her breasts to his chest, flexed his hips and forged inside her. Her flesh fluttered around his hardness, delight searing from every inch he stretched beyond its limits. Once buried inside her, he stilled at the gate of her womb. Twisting his long-healed hand in her wet hair, he withdrew so agonizingly slowly.

He whispered as he thrust back, his voice the deepest, darkest spell it had ever been.

"You're mine, Eliana. Mine to pleasure. Mine to protect. Mine to love." He nudged her very heart. *"Mine."*

That was all it took. Her core spasmed over his hardness in the exquisite scalding of release. Baring his teeth, a harsh hiss flayed her cheek as he unleashed his pleasure inside her, marking her, mastering her, intensifying her orgasm. She shook against him, eyes clinging to his as he finished her.

Long after she lay in his arms quivering, body replete, heart shattered, he gently withdrew from her depths, then finished cleaning her. Taking her out of the shower, he dried her off and carried her to bed.

Gathering her in his arms under the covers, he kissed her all over her face, his caressing hand moving down to her belly. "You're carrying my child."

She huffed weakly. "Whatever tipped you off?"

His gorgeous lips twitched. "The morning sickness fest just confirmed it…but I've been noticing changes in your body." He tasted her nipples, sent pleasure forking through her to lodge in her womb. "Those delights are becoming thicker, darker, and they give you even more pleasure when I do this." He suckled each hotly, had her arching helplessly, surrendering her flesh to his mastery. "You're also more responsive, when I thought that impossible, igniting into a conflagration much more quickly."

"That's just your overachiever self. You taught my body to expect more pleasure each time, until you had it perpetually ready to go off at a touch."

Her confession was rewarded by a look of supreme male satisfaction before he rose off the bed, knowing what the sight of his arousal would do to her.

Striding into the bathroom, she heard him rustling around. Then he rejoined her, took her hand and slipped his ring again on her finger.

Looking down at her, he pressed her hand to his heart. "You'll never take my ring off, never leave my side again. I let you go only so you could calm down, but I won't let you do this to yourself. Take your anguish out on me, never on yourself." At her miserable silence, he gritted his teeth. "Weren't you going to tell me about the baby?"

"Don't you know me at all?" she countered.

His eyes softened with such…adoration. It still felt like the most genuine thing she'd ever known.

"I know all of you. It's why you have all of me." Pain entered his gaze. "You must have found out yesterday, must have been coming to tell me when you overheard us."

As always, he just knew. It had been how he'd manipulated her so seamlessly. "Yeah, I arrived just in time to hear them congratulating you on the adjustment of your plan."

"If you'd waited you would have heard me blasting them for refusing to believe you were never part of my plan and forbidding them to ever mention you again. Richard is the only one who knows what we have together, and he knew they'd stepped on forbidden territory." She did remember Graves saying something to that effect. "But I don't care what they think. I only care about you. I'm here to take you home, *meu amor*."

"I can't…I can't be with you anymore."

"You were just with me now. And you'll always be with me."

"You know what this was. I'm unable to resist you, but it will kill me to be with you now."

"Don't ever say things like that. I'll give you time to come to terms with all this on the condition you never shut me out again."

"I'm more valuable now that I'm a dual-purpose instrument, right? A weapon in your revenge, and a vessel for you heir." Before he voiced his thunderous disapproval of her interpretation, a terrible idea sparked in her mind. A bargain. "But I will do everything you wish, Rafael…if you let your plan to destroy my father go. Whatever that would cost you, I will compensate you."

He sat up, the animosity she'd always felt and he'd hidden so well on full blast now. "There's no compensating me for what your father did. And don't ask what that was. I already told you it has nothing to do with you. And it will remain so."

Giving up, she left the bed on shaking legs and went to retrieve her clothes. Once she'd pulled on the clean layers, she exited the bathroom to find him blocking her way.

Circumventing him, she stopped at the door. "I can't stop you, Rafael. But I can stop myself."

He prowled toward her. "You can't. You will never stop loving me, just as I will never stop loving you till the day I die."

"Even if I never do, it makes no difference. What we had, whatever that was, is over."

"It will never be over between us, Eliana. You'll always be mine to protect and cherish every second of my life. And I will be there for every second of your pregnancy, and our child will be born with us long married."

His conviction overwhelmed her. Warding off another wave of nausea, she staggered past him.

She was at the door when he said something else, so calm and final, it made her stumble the rest of the away out of the hotel.

Once outside, she found Daniel there, waiting. In no condition to refuse his services, she entered the luxurious, perfectly air-conditioned limo, slumped in her seat and closed her eyes, Rafael's last words looping in her mind, deepening her desperation.

He'd said, "Our wedding will take place on time."

Knowing it was pointless to keep running from Rafael, that he'd only keep coming after her, Ellie returned to the mansion. But she drew the line at sharing his bed.

He let her choose where she'd stay. She chose the suite as far away from him as possible on ground level, and she was relieved he didn't try to invade it once she sought its refuge. He was apparently giving her time to "come to terms," as he'd called it.

But there was no doing that while she mistrusted his motives, didn't know the secret behind his enmity and expected a catastrophe to befall her father at any moment.

After another day in hell, longing for him and knowing it was a futile effort to again demand he tell her everything, realization descended on her like a hammer.

She knew who could tell her the truth.

His brothers.

For all their ruthlessness, Ellie was certain Graves, Raiden and Numair loved Rafael.

At least to the extent that those men *could* love. She bet, whatever they felt, they wouldn't further jeopardize his plans if they could at all help it.

So she demanded to meet them, threatening that if they told Rafael, it would be on their heads when she left him standing at the altar.

Since Raiden and Numair didn't think much of her, they couldn't risk her carrying out her threat and complied. Graves didn't believe her for a second, but followed suit anyway.

After resorting to elaborate maneuvers to throw Rafael's surveillance off, she now sat in Graves's ocean-facing penthouse suite at the Copacabana Palace Hotel. Looking at those three Olympians who sat across from her like some ancient tribunal that would decide her fate, she wondered again how they had so much in common with Rafael.

It felt as if they'd been forged in the same merciless crucible, molded into the same brand of lethal weapon.

Raiden was coolly assessing her, as if deciding on an attack strategy. She had no doubt that when he struck, he did so out of nowhere and turned his opponents to ashes, as his code name, Lightning, suggested.

Numair—Phantom—was every bit his code name, too, chilling, elusive and impossible to fathom. With him no one knew where they stood, and she had a feeling that made him the deadliest of all.

Graves was looking at her with the tolerance someone would have for a posturing cat that didn't realize it wasn't so much intimidating as endearing.

She finally sat forward. "Got enough of sizing me up?" When the men just continued staring at her, she blew out a breath. "To business, then. As you so kindly shattered my illusions the other night, you now must finish your task and tell me what Rafael won't."

Graves shook his head. "Let it go. Knowing the truth would only hurt you."

"Is there more hurt than knowing the man I love— the father of my baby—is using me to send my father to prison?"

The men looked at each other. The baby was news to them. So Rafael did consider her forbidden territory he shared with no one. But she felt a baby somehow changed everything to them. The shift in their attitude was almost palpable.

"There is always more hurt, Ms. Ferreira," Numair said in that hair-raising sereneness. "Some snake pits are better left closed forever."

She gave a mirthless huff. "Well, this one is wide-open, and serpents have been slithering out all over me. I know you're here because you'd rather spare Rafael further trouble with me. But if he thinks this is hurting me less, I'm telling you he's wrong. I can't live with not knowing."

Another eloquent glance passed between the men before Graves finally sat forward. It seemed they'd elected him to be their spokesman.

Holding her breath, knowing what she was about to hear

would change everything, she hung on to his every word as he started talking.

And she finally understood what they'd meant by saying there was always more hurt. This was a level beyond her worst nightmares.

What happened to Rafael, to all of them, the suffering they'd had to endure… It was beyond her worst nightmares.

Numbness spread in her every cell, an attempt to ward off the horror, to protect her psyche from being torn apart. Imagining Rafael as a child, taken and imprisoned, abused and broken…it was…it was… No way to describe, to take in, to bear…

Ellie's eyes fluttered open.

Jackknifing to a sitting position, the whole world heaved around her, making her collapse back. On a bed. It had to be Graves's hotel bed.

"Dammit," she moaned as she struggled to sit up. Hands on both sides helped her. Raiden's and Numair's. "I've never even felt dizzy all my life, and now I faint every weekday."

"You must promise *you'll* never tell Rafael of this." Graves's intimidating face came into wavering focus as he stood at the foot of the bed. "He can't find out you were in my bed, under any circumstances. I'm fond of certain anatomical parts."

She looked up at him, at the other two, and tears gushed from her depths.

The men's consternation rose as sobs almost tore her apart before their eyes. These men who'd vanquished the world's evils had no way of dealing with a woman's tears. As they fidgeted and exchanged anxious glances, it was clear they would have rather been dealing with a ticking bomb.

But she couldn't help it. The more she imagined the atrocities that had befallen Rafael all those years ago, the more violent her weeping became.

Her distress soon overpowered the men's ability to withstand it, and they took refuge in action. Swarming around her, she found herself propped by pillows from all sides, and they were blotting her tears, bathing her burning face in cold compresses, warming her freezing hands in heated ones and offering her every comfort food and drink that existed in Rio.

Limp with anguish, she surrendered to their ministrations, all but the dietary one. At the first warning heave, they rushed to take ingestible stuff away. She had a feeling they would rather get shot than deal with *that*.

It felt like hours before she was finally drained of all her tears, and lay there barely managing the in-out motions of breathing. The men seemed just as depleted, sitting around the bed as if they'd been through a thirty-round fight with a gorilla.

"Please tell us you're done crying," Raiden groaned.

Her breath hitched. As they all tensed again, she only nodded. There was nothing more in her. For now.

Exhaling in relief, Graves said, "How is it possible a woman your size has all that water in her?"

"Speaking of water." Raiden grimaced at the memory as he fetched a carafe. "You need to replace the rivers you lost."

Contradictorily the one who looked most rattled by her weeping storm, Numair warned, "Sip it slowly. Otherwise, you might choke. Or throw up. Or both. Or do some other catastrophic thing. Like burst into another crying jag."

As she did as instructed, Numair regarded her heavily. "That was for Rafael. You can't bear imagining what he's been through."

Her breath hitched again. "And that I can't do anything about it."

Numair exchanged a look with Raiden. Then he shook his head. "You *do* love him."

She looked at both men through almost swollen-shut lids. "You figured this out on your own?"

And she saw what she'd thought impossible. A semblance of a smile on Numair's cruel lips. "It was a long-shot deduction."

Suddenly, it all crashed into place. "Rafael thinks my father had a hand in his abduction!"

Exchanging another of those glances, and making another decision, Numair was the one who told her the details.

This time there were no tears. Just conviction. It made her sit up steady. "No way my father did that!"

Raiden shrugged. "Rafael has evidence."

Slumping back with this new blow, she felt her world churning.

Graves, who'd been silent for a while, came forward, checking her temperature.

She clung to his hand. "I need to know more."

Another shared glance between the men, then Graves asked, "What do you need to know?"

"These aren't your real names."

He shook his head. "They are our names now."

"How did Rafael pick his name?"

"He was wounded on a mission. Bones, our medical expert, performed a desperate field surgery on him, removed his kidney and spleen to stem his internal bleeding, thinking he'd die anyway. But he recovered fully as if by an act of God."

"Rafael. *God has healed...*"

At Graves's nod, another sob tore her. That scar. She'd felt it resonate with such…pain, such…loss. She'd been right. Oh, God, Rafael…all he'd lost, all he'd survived…

"He picked Moreno Salazar," Raiden said. "*Dark old house,* just as I chose Kuroshiro, which means *black castle* in Japanese, as a sort of twisted tribute to our being the product of this ancient, sinister place where we were imprisoned and created."

"Before you told me all that," she whispered, "I was thinking you did feel as if you've been forged in the same hell."

"I'm beginning to see why Rafael fell for you," Raiden said, that assessment in his eyes tinged with approval.

"He didn't. He was just using me."

Graves waved her words away as if they were rubbish. "He fell for you. All the way. I was there that first night he did. I can't begin to explain how it happened, but it certainly did." At her mournful disbelief, he growled, "Bloody hell, the man went prematurely gray with fright over you. What more proof do you need?"

Silver *had* appeared in his temples after her accident. Rafael had waved the coincidence away, but she'd believed it just the same...until she'd overheard that fateful conversation. Believing it again, believing he loved her, made things worse not better.

Shying away from the implications, she sought a diversion. "If Rafael is Brazilian by birth, why didn't he make Brazil his base of operations all along?"

"His homeland was always the one place he didn't want to be," Numair explained. "He's one of only three of us who know their family, but when we first escaped, he couldn't contact his, fearing the Organization might be keeping them under surveillance in case he returned to them. Then he found that his parents got divorced after his abduction, remarried and had more children. But even when we established our new identities, he didn't want to disrupt their lives all over again."

That was also what he'd told her, just without the compelling reasons that had stopped him from seeking his family again. It hadn't been a choice but a necessity that had been forced on him.

"He thought he'd become someone totally different from the boy they'd lost," Graves said. "He still believes they're better off not knowing the man he's become. For years, he watched them from afar, but I guess I wore him down because he finally reentered their lives a couple of years ago. Though the stubborn boy only did so with his new identity and remains a peripheral acquaintance."

Even when he'd finally sought his family, he settled for the comfort of seeing them up close…as a stranger.

"But he's in Brazil now as some sort of poetic justice," Raiden interjected. "Because this was where he was taken, where it started, and it's where he wants to exact his revenge, where he wants it to end."

That fist perpetually wringing her heart tightened.

This was all beyond comprehension, beyond endurance. Even if he'd manipulated her, he had an overwhelming reason for it. What had been done to him had been monstrous, unforgiveable, irreparable.

But it couldn't have been her father who'd done it.

It couldn't.

"Rafael…"

He could swear he'd felt Eliana the moment she'd thought of seeking him. But he'd curbed the urge to stampede toward her. If she didn't give herself voluntarily, it would mean nothing.

But she was seeking him now, standing there on his threshold looking as if she was in deep mourning.

"I know everything."

He rose slowly to his feet, gritting his teeth on the surge of dismay. "I'll skin them alive."

She approached, and it took all the self-restraint he had not to obliterate the distance and crush her in his arms.

"I insisted I wouldn't go through with the wedding if they didn't tell me." She stopped two feet away, red-rimmed eyes filled with a world of pain, reproach and...empathy? "You were wrong to hide the truth from me."

"I'd rather you hate me than your father." Surprise flitted across her pale, haggard face. Apparently, that motive hadn't even occurred to her. "I thought I'd manage to break through your resentment in time, but I didn't want the world you've built on your belief in your father to come crashing down. Even when I punished him, I wanted you to continue thinking of me as the villain, not him."

She surged forward, gripped his arms. Even though her touch was distraught, it felt like sustenance when he was starving.

"But you have to be wrong, Rafael. My father isn't a villain. And he would die before he harmed a child."

Her butchered protest told him if he insisted to the contrary, he risked sundering what remained of their tenuous emotional bond.

Everything inside her had been damaged; everything between them hung by a thread. She was still unable to stop loving or wanting him, but it was still possible he'd exacerbate her injuries, making them incurable, and end up losing her altogether.

He'd die before he did.

There was only one venue open to him now.

He took it. "I'm open to giving your father every benefit of the doubt, and to uncovering new evidence. However long it may take to find it. Is that acceptable to you?"

And this being who was everything to him looked at him with those eyes that were his world and nodded.

He crushed her in his arms at last, her feel reclaiming him from the wasteland of separation.

"Will you marry me now?"

Eleven

Eliana had agreed to resume their wedding plans.

But it seemed her faith in his feelings was still damaged, or at least hadn't recovered yet. There had been no return to intimacy between them.

Rafael couldn't push. Not when everything inside her felt doused, no matter how passionate and attentive he was. All he could think was that she still thought everything he did for her was self-serving, that she continued to think herself an instrument to serve his purposes. First vengeance and now the child he couldn't wait to have, a child to give the life he'd been deprived of.

There was nothing he could do but continue to love her and hope time would prove to her what pledges never could.

Ellie rushed through Rafael's expansive, exquisite mansion, inspecting the guest suites for readiness.

The wedding was tomorrow. And her half brothers were flying in from the States, while all of Rafael's brothers were coming over for the wedding rehearsal. They'd all be spending the night in the mansion.

Rafael had left it up to her to distribute their guests. He continued to give her carte blanche with everything. Not that this made her feel anywhere near the lady of the mansion. While before she'd felt at least at home here, she now felt like a trespasser, and wondered if that feeling would ever go away.

For now she had to focus on making sure everything was ready for their families' arrival. She'd assigned the poolside suites to them. Some of the suites had panoramic views of the ocean, gardens, waterfalls and the hillside plunging deeply into Ferradura Bay. Others were tucked away, opened to the lush botanical gardens, sparkling lagoons and cascading waterfalls.

But none had the stunning three-hundred-and-sixty-degree views, open-air shower, sundeck and spa of Rafael's master suite. What used to be *theirs,* and would be so again starting tomorrow night.

But how could she share his personal space and bed again? Although he'd said he'd consider new evidence, how could she possibly find any? And even with him putting his revenge plans on hold, what kind of life would they have with all of this between them? His initial duplicity, his unresolved animosity toward her father, her unabated fear he'd act on it?

Unable to think any further than today, she went about the mind-emptying chores of stocking all the suites with Rafael's legion of hired help.

Starting tomorrow night, the rest of her life as Rafael's wife and the mother of his child would begin. And the idea struck her at once with joy...and despondence.

In the southern gardens overlooking the Atlantic, Rafael stood watching Eliana as she walked toward him down the aisle with her father, the man who'd sentenced him to hell.

It was only a rehearsal. Only the people who had a role in the ceremony were there. Others, like her half brothers and Ferreira's PA, Isabella Da Costa, would be coming tomorrow. But everything with her always felt like the real thing. The only thing that mattered.

And as she approached him in her flowing pistachio dress, her hair swept up in that ponytail it had become one of his life's keenest pleasures to undo, he felt his being well up with love for her.

Her eyes embraced his all the way, so much emotion filling them. He was beside himself being unable to read it all. Then she was a breath away, and that man he'd hated for so long, even before he'd known his identity, was giving him her hand.

He looked at Ferreira for a long moment…and suddenly realized.

He was no longer angry.

He no longer cared about anything. Nothing mattered to him anymore. Nothing but her.

Though this rehearsal was about going through the motions, getting the sequence flowing smoothly, and he wouldn't be saying his actual vows until tomorrow, he couldn't wait until then to share his epiphany with her.

So he took her hands to his lips, to his heart. "Eliana, my every answer to my every prayer…I'm letting go of everything, my heart. I cling only to your love, want nothing but your happiness and peace of mind, *meu coração*."

Rafael's pledge had been the last thing Ellie had expected from him. It had been reverberating inside her ever since, knocking down every barrier, ending every uncertainty.

Unable to wait to be alone with him, she gazed at him as the rehearsal came to an end, her heart shedding its sluggish despondence, back to the hammering of anticipation.

As he hugged another three men, the rest of his brothers—

minus one all were loath to talk about—she couldn't really see anything but him.

Dressed in all black, he'd lost weight in the past two weeks. It only made him seem taller, his shoulders and chest even wider in comparison to the sparser waist and hips. His face was hewn to sharper planes and angles, his skin a darker, silkier copper, intensifying the luminescence of his eyes. The discreet silver in his luxurious raven hair, that testament to his absolute love, added the last touch of allure.

Then she was swept up in his arms among his brothers' hoots and hollers that he was disgracing them by anticipating the wedding night. Not in a condition to be embarrassed, she clung to him all the way to their quarters.

But the moment he placed her on the bed and came down beside her, her disquiet returned.

Twisting her ponytail around his wrist, harnessing her by it, ferocity barely leashed by gentleness, he tilted up her face. "No more distance, *minha vida,* ever again."

"That's not it…I just—just… Oh, God, please, Rafael, show me your evidence against my father."

His face settled in adamant lines. "I *have* given this up. I consider anything I've been through the path to finding you. You remember when you said you'd compensate me? Finding you is more compensation than I've ever dreamed I could have."

"But what you have against him is airtight, right?"

"This is what I was afraid of, for your faith in him to be irrevocably damaged, causing you this much pain."

Her chest ached, her eyes burned. "Everything in me rebels against believing any such thing of my father, but it isn't why I'm in agony. It's for you. What you suffered was unthinkable."

"It's in the past."

"But this is the present and future. How can I share my life and body and baby with you if there's even the slightest possibility my father committed such an unforgivable crime against you? Even if he had done so under unspeakable duress? Throwing you in hell while he lavished his love on me?" She released a shuddering breath. "Even if you've decided to look the other way for my sake and that of our lives together, *I* can't. I can't live believing one of the two people my life has been built around did the other such unimaginable injury, for whatever reason."

After a long moment, he said, "Do you believe in your heart your father didn't do it—or at least was forced to do it somehow?"

She nodded. "But I can't even begin to think how this could have happened."

"Then that's it. I'm now ready to disbelieve anything but the verdict of your heart. It's never wrong. That heart saw through the hatred cloaking mine, blew away my bitterness and anger, made me experience what I never thought I was capable of—a love without bounds. I trust your heart, and only your heart."

She gaped at him, unable to take that much love.

He had more to give. "I'll do anything to find new evidence in your father's favor. To that end, if you permit, I want to face him. He's the only one who might provide missing information needed to paint a truer picture."

It terrified her that a confrontation might provide definitive proof that her father's reasons hadn't been overwhelming enough. But knowing this must be resolved, she consented. But on one condition.

"If it turns out my father did what you think he did and had no acceptable reason for his actions, I want you to deal with him as you see fit, to make no more allowances for his being my father. You have to have justice…and closure."

Not intending to ever fulfill that condition, Rafael escorted Eliana to her father's suite.

The man, who'd already gone to bed, seemed to think he wasn't quite awake when Rafael told him who he really was.

His expression changed from blank, to flabbergasted— then he shot up and pounced on Rafael.

He pulled back, tears in his eyes. "*Deus,* could it really be you? Oh, *meu caro*...your disappearance hit me almost as hard as it hit your parents. The indescribable loss brought me back to your father's side after we had our stupid falling out and I was idiotically sulking. He clung to my support during the search for you, but then your case was closed. We turned the world upside down looking for you on our own, but once your father became certain you were lost to him, he pulled away from everyone." Deep sorrow creased his face. "It was why he and your mother divorced. They dealt with their grief in different ways and couldn't find their way back to one another. I tried to keep in touch with him, but he couldn't bear knowing anyone from the life that had you in it."

From Ferreira's reaction, Rafael no longer doubted he'd had *anything* to do with his abduction. Which left only one explanation. The real culprit had left the threads of evidence that would lead to Ferreira, clues that had been so ingenious, the police had missed all of them, and only he with his abilities and reach had found them twenty-four years later.

Eliana told her father Rafael had thought he was the one who'd orchestrated his abduction, and Ferreira's dumb-founded reaction solidified his belief in the man's innocence.

Looking relieved beyond measure, she sought his confirmation, and he rushed to give it to her. "It wasn't him, *meu amor.* As always, your heart is my compass."

After a clinging, tearful kiss, she turned to her father. "Do you have any idea who could have framed you, Daddy?"

Ferreira looked dazedly from his daughter to Rafael, obviously struggling to readjust to everything he thought he knew of the past months since Rafael had entered their lives.

Then Ferreira burst out in belated affront, "You're telling me all this time you thought it was me? You came here to punish me? That's why you went after Ellie?"

"I wasn't part of his plan, Daddy."

Relief and pride spread though Rafael. Her faith in him had been healed, and was back to the purity he now depended on.

"Eliana is why everything was put right," he said gruffly. "Her love pulled me back from the path of destruction and into a life I never thought I'd have. But I need you to think. Anything you can remember around that time would help. It had to be someone who was close to you. Think, Ferreira."

The man blinked numbly. Then he said, "You used to call me Tio Teo."

"I used to love you almost as much as I loved my father." He tried to smile through the pain stabbing in his chest. "But I don't think I can call you that now."

Eliana kissed his shoulder. "How about only Teo?"

Looking down at her, his heart in his eyes, he pledged, "Whatever you wish, *minha alma*."

Suddenly, Teo grabbed his arm. "There's something. When I first met Ellie's mother, she had a stalker. I hired a security specialist to deal with the situation until that stalker was caught. I can't think of anyone else in my whole life who had the kind of skills and underground connections needed to do something like…like…"

Ferreira fell silent, eyes feverish as he chased new realizations, connected seemingly unconnected events.

Then he focused back on Rafael. "He must have realized through me that you were just what that organization was looking for, and he'd had all the access to me he needed to doctor evidence to incriminate me."

"Give me his name."

After Ferreira did so, Rafael rose to his feet and bent to kiss Eliana. "I'll initiate a targeted investigation at once."

"Thank you, *meu amor*," she whispered against his lips.

"Anything and everything for you, *minha vida*. Always."

In an hour, Rafael walked back into his father-in-law's suite. He stopped at the door, savoring the sight of the love of his life curled into her father, with his arm around her and their heads nestled against each other.

Overpowering emotions swept him. And not only for Eliana. But for her father, too. He was again the uncle he'd loved, but now far more, the man whose adoration for his wife had given him Eliana, a being made of total love.

Blinking back the burn behind his eyes, he walked in. And, oh…the welcome, the warmth, he saw on both their faces! He felt any lingering pain and bitterness and rage just drain away.

He came down on his haunches before them, delighting in how Eliana surged forward and took him in her arms, pressing his head to her heart.

"Thank you for believing Daddy, *meu amor*. Even if you can't find proof, it's enough you want to."

"Found anything?" Teo asked anxiously.

Rafael pulled back from her embrace to look at him. "Once I had a name and a connection to you, everything fell…or rather crashed into place. I traced the man's every move and contact and bank account transaction since the day I was abducted. And there's no doubt. It *was* him."

Eliana's choking cry shook his heartstrings as she pulled them both to her, buried her face in their chests in turn and soaked them in her tears of relief.

His own relief was even fiercer, and all for her, that she didn't have to live with something this horrible standing between the two people she loved most, that she wouldn't feel guilty about his ordeals anymore.

After they both kissed and soothed her, he reached for Teo's hand, squeezed it. "I beg your forgiveness, Teo, for believing in your guilt once my investigations led to you. I didn't want it to be you, but when I dug again and again to make sure, I kept finding the same trails."

Teo squeezed his hand back. "It was impossible for you to realize that man's involvement. Anita was so scared of the whole thing, I couldn't tell anyone, even your father." He sighed in regret. "Ironically, it was the massive expenses of hiring that man, and which I couldn't account for, that led to your father dissolving our partnership. And then I lost her, then your father…and that man disappeared from my memory."

His viciousness now targeted the man who'd cost him so much, and who'd almost made him destroy innocent lives. "You don't need to ever think of him again. He's already… being taken care of."

Teo's eyes widened. "You mean you…?"

Eliana clutched her father's arm, cold fire arcing from her eyes. "Rafael will make sure he never hurts anyone else. And that he gets what he deserves."

Teo's surprise at the blade in Eliana's tone was nothing compared to Rafael's. Delight soared as he pulled her closer.

"So my made-for-and-from-love flower can be deadly when defending and avenging the innocent."

The flames in her eyes licked his every nerve. "You bet."

He cocked an eyebrow at her, wanting to see how far she'd go. "So you condone anything I choose to do to that man?"

Her lush lips hardened. "He's no man. He's a monster. And you and your brothers are monster slayers. I know whatever you choose to do to him will be the right thing to do."

Joy swelled inside him as he pulled her closer again. "Have you told Teo our news?"

Her eyes drained of righteous wrath, flooded with shyness. "I didn't ask if you wanted to let anyone know."

Throwing his head back, he guffawed. "'Anyone' didn't

include those six huge pains who've been teasing the hell out of me all day with parenting jokes, huh?"

A fiery flush spread across her exquisite cheekbones. "I sort of let it slip to your trio of terror while I was milking them for info." She mumbled something about poking his blabbing brothers with sharp objects when next she saw them. "And they ran with the news to the rest of the roster!"

"You're pregnant?"

Teo's explosive exclamation snapped their eyes to him, and he threw an arm around each of them, exalting, "I'm going to be a grandfather!"

Eliana kissed him soundly. "I know you've given up on the others and think I'm your only chance at grandbabies. But you're not going to have only one grandchild, but two."

Surprise was now Teo's only expression. "You're having twins? Is it even possible to know that early?"

Eliana got Rafael's silent consent before turning to her father. "We're going to adopt Diego."

Teo slumped back. "Any more monumental, life-changing surprises? Just pour them down on me all at once."

Rafael chuckled again. "That's enough for now."

"More than enough for a lifetime." Teo's eyes filled. "If I die right this moment, I'll be the happiest man on earth."

Rafael gave him a mock-stern look. "Now, Teo, let's not restart our relationship on the wrong foot. The happiest man on earth is me. Got that?"

"If you say so." Teo gave the acquiescing sigh of a man who was letting a younger man think he had his way.

Laughing outright this time, Rafael swept his hugely grinning, teary-eyed bride up in his arms. "I do. Oh, how I do."

"I certainly don't!"

Ellie laughed as her eldest half brother, Leonardo, vehemently denied that he liked having those seminaked photos of him leaked online. They'd gone viral with half the globe's females drooling over him and captioning them no end.

"All those straining muscles and the pouring sweat and provocative poses?" Santiago winked at them. Her middle half brother relished how his looks affected anything that moved, not like Leonardo, the scientist who wanted his brains to be his prominent feature. "No way those masterpieces were without your consent."

"I was exercising," Leonardo growled. "And since when are chest flies, squats and one-armed push-ups provocative poses?"

"*Have* you seen the photos, Leo?" Ellie giggled.

Leonardo harrumphed. "Phones with cameras and the internet will bring civilization to an end."

"Just enjoy the notoriety, Leonardo. It's harmless." Rafael's lips twisted. "I hope."

Leonardo looked at him gratefully. "*Thank you* for recognizing the world is full of nuts."

Suddenly worried, Ellie caught Leonardo's forearm. "Did anyone do anything nutty?"

Leonardo rolled his eyes. "Apart from walking into the lecture hall and finding hearts and chocolate all over the counter or the collection of panties spirited into my briefcase with photos and phone numbers stuck on them? No."

As they all laughed, Carlos, her youngest half brother, and her closest sibling slapped him on the back. "And you didn't share your crop of panties with your brothers?"

Leonardo scowled at him. "Shouldn't you be exporting panties, given the way women throw themselves at you?"

Carlos shuddered. "Not when I've perfected the art of dodging feminine missiles. Unlike you, I don't stand still long enough for them to stuff panties in my personal effects."

As everyone laughed again, Ellie felt euphoric.

After treating the news of Rafael's real identity and his

history with due gravity, her half brothers had proceeded to seamlessly treat him as an old childhood friend, and their very welcome new brother-in-law.

Suddenly, she felt Rafael tense. After looking at his phone, he made their excuses to her brothers.

Heart thudding, she turned away with him and crossed the garden overlooking the ocean where they would have their ceremony. As they rushed, she was again thankful for her both functional and pretty wedding dress—white as snow, embroidered in pearls and sequins, chiffon and satin with a strapless, pleated bodice and a flowing, easy-to-run-in skirt.

Not that *she* could run. "Easy, *amor*."

At her wince, Rafael slowed down at once. They'd ended the previous night by going to bed. After the two weeks of turmoil and alienation, the discharge of passion had been cataclysmic. She was deliciously sore after he'd ravished her again and again, as she'd pleaded for him to, and had spent the day struggling to walk straight.

They reentered the mansion from its western entrance, and her pulse raced with anticipation as they neared the man and woman who stood rooted in the middle of the foyer.

His parents.

She'd begged him to contact them, to let them know that the son they thought they'd lost was alive and well and incredibly happy. She couldn't bear knowing they existed, had that permanent scar of his loss and would not be given the choice to reconnect with him. He'd finally succumbed to her wishes and called them.

His parents, especially his father, had been distraught.

Asking them not to tell anyone until they figured out a safe way to introduce him to his siblings, he'd asked them to attend their wedding. Both he and Numair had sent their private jets to fetch them from their homes in Fortaleza and

Belém. They'd postponed the ceremony to around sunset until his parents could arrive.

Now Rafael was face-to-face with them. Though they'd both known Rafael for the past two years, they'd only known him as his new persona. Now they saw him as their long-lost son come back to life.

It felt surreal to Ellie, meeting his father, Andrés Ríos Navarro, who was also her father's once-best friend. Bianca Franco Molena, his mother, had once been her mother's friend, too.

"I'm so sorry…" Andrés blurted out, swallowed, then he burst into tears. Rafael's mother followed suit.

Rafael pulled his father into a fierce hug. "I'm the one who's sorry I didn't tell you before." He dragged his mother into the hug, and let them weep for all the years of helplessness, dread and heartache as he enclosed them in his power and protection.

When their emotional storm abated, Rafael reached out to Ellie. She rushed to join them in his all-encompassing embrace.

Kissing them all, he smiled gently at his parents, and adoringly at her. "You owe my coming to my senses to my bride, the one who put everything in my life right."

And Ellie found herself in his parents' arms, squeezed and kissed and thanked for the miracle of having their son back.

"It's me who thanks you for giving me the only man I'll ever love," she choked out. "But has he told you my full name?"

Both blinked at her uncomprehendingly. After she told them, they gaped. Then they burst out talking at once.

"Teo's daughter?"

"How is that even possible?"

"Where is Teo?"

"Is he here?"

She hooked her arm into theirs and steered them out to the garden. "He is here, and he's been waiting all my life to see you again."

Their ceremony went without a hitch, and sort of felt like an afterthought. Apart from Rafael's parents meeting her father, and Rafael pulling her father into his embrace as he gave him her hand, and her father finally exchanging his first kiss with Isabella in jubilation after her and Rafael's "I dos," all the monumental stuff had already happened during and after the rehearsal yesterday.

Everyone had retired to their suites after long hours of celebration, and she was in Rafael's arms again. And she couldn't hold her tears back again.

"*Deus, coração,* I can't see your tears even if they're ones of joy...." Then he exclaimed, "Those aren't tears of joy!"

"I'm sorry, *meu amor,* but I don't know if I'll ever finish weeping for the boy you were, for what you lost."

"With what I've gained—you, our coming baby, Diego and even more brothers—I am now obscenely blessed. I even got back everything I lost—my parents, with their new broods sure to follow them. And Teo." He pulled her with him to a reclining position and she burrowed deeper into his chest. "And together we will give our baby and Diego everything I was deprived of, and what even you didn't have, both a mother and father." Suddenly he squeezed her tight. "Who won't let them out of their sights!"

Laughing through the tears, she spluttered, "Don't you go smothering our baby and Diego with love!"

His lips twisted. "Any complaints yourself?"

"Hmm, you've got a point." She pulled him on top of her. "Smother me some more."

"Sorceress." His chuckle poured into her lips.

But as he started making love to her, lightness drained as her hand feathered his scar.

"I wish I had real magic, *meu amor*. I would have erased this scar, its memory and all the memories of your suffering."

"You already have. You found me, *saw* me for what I am. You made me yours and healed all my wounds and erased all my scars." He joined their bodies, swallowed her cry. "Now you'll love me forever. You don't only have magic. You *are* magic."

She wrapped herself around him, inside and out, took him to the very heart of her, and whispered, "Look who's talking…."

* * * * *

If you loved
FROM ENEMY'S DAUGHTER TO EXPECTANT BRIDE,
pick up the next book in USA TODAY *bestselling author*
Olivia Gates's series
THE BILLIONAIRES OF BLACK CASTLE

SCANDALOUSLY EXPECTING HIS CHILD
Coming December 2014!

Also available now from Olivia Gates:
TEMPORARILY HIS PRINCESS
CONVENIENTLY HIS PRINCESS
CLAIMING HIS OWN
SEDUCING HIS PRINCESS
THE SARANTOS BABY BARGAIN

REQUEST YOUR FREE BOOKS!
2 FREE NOVELS PLUS 2 FREE GIFTS!

Here's a sneak peek of
THE SECRET AFFAIR
by New York Times *and* USA TODAY *bestselling author*
Brenda Jackson

Dr. Aidan Westmoreland entered his apartment and re-moved his lab coat. After running a hand down his face, he glanced at his watch, frustrated. He'd hoped he would have heard something by now. What if…

The ringing of his cell phone made him pause. It was the call he'd been waiting for. "Paige?"

"Yes, it's me."

"Is Jillian still going?" he asked, not wasting time with chitchat.

There was a slight pause on the other end, and in that short space of time knots formed in his stomach. "Yes, she's still going on the cruise, Aidan."

He released the breath he'd been holding as Paige con-tinued, "Jill still has no idea I'm aware that the two of you had an affair."

Aidan hadn't known Paige knew the truth either, until she'd paid him a surprise visit last month. According to her, she'd figured things out the year Jillian had entered medical school. She'd become suspicious when he'd come home for his cousin Riley's wedding and she'd overheard him call Jillian Jilly in an intimate tone. Paige had been concerned this past year when she'd noticed

Jillian seemed troubled by something that she wouldn't share with Paige.

Paige had talked to Ivy, Jillian's best friend, who'd also been concerned about Jillian. Ivy had shared everything about the situation with Paige. Which had prompted Paige to fly to Charlotte and confront him. Until then, Aidan had been clueless as to the real reason behind his and Jillian's breakup.

When Paige had told him about the cruise she and Jillian had planned and she'd suggested an idea for getting Jillian on the cruise alone, he'd readily embraced it.

"I've done my part and the rest is up to you, Aidan. I hope you can convince Jill of the truth."

Moments later he ended the call and continued to the kitchen, where he grabbed a beer. Two weeks on the open seas with Jillian would be interesting. But he intended to make it more than just interesting. He aimed to make it productive.

A determined smile spread across his lips. By the time the cruise ended there would be no doubt in Jillian's mind that he was the only man for her.

*Find out how this secret affair began—and how
Aidan plans to claim his woman in
THE SECRET AFFAIR by New York Times and
USA TODAY bestselling author Brenda Jackson.*

*Available December 2014,
wherever Harlequin® Desire books and ebooks are sold!*

HARLEQUIN®

Desire

ALWAYS POWERFUL, PASSIONATE AND PROVOCATIVE.

USA TODAY bestselling author
Janice Maynard
Brings you the next installment of
The Kavanaghs of Silver Glen

CHRISTMAS IN THE BILLIONAIRE'S BED

Available December 2014

'Tis the season for a steamy reunion for past lovers...

Whatever possessed Emma Braithwaite to move
to Silver Glen? She had no illusions that being in
Aidan Kavanagh's hometown would reignite their
love. But now that Aidan's returned for his brother's
Christmas wedding, it's clear her explosive attraction
to him has lost none of its power.

She is the cool English beauty whose betrayal once
shattered his heart. So Aidan's not looking for
reconciliation—all he wants is Emma in his bed!
Needless to say, Emma has other ideas: she's not settling
for anything less than commitment this time...

Don't miss other exciting titles from Janice Maynard's
The Kavanaghs of Silver Glen:

BABY FOR KEEPS
A NOT-SO-INNOCENT SEDUCTION

Available wherever books and ebooks are sold.

HD733576

HARLEQUIN®

Desire

ALWAYS POWERFUL, PASSIONATE AND PROVOCATIVE.

USA TODAY bestselling author

Olivia Gates

brings you the next installment of

The Billionaires of Black Castle miniseries

SCANDALOUSLY EXPECTING HIS CHILD

Available December 2014

Will he renounce his birthright for the woman who carries his child?

Self-made billionaire Raiden Kuroshiro escaped a dark past vowing to reclaim his heritage. But when the woman who once betrayed him returns, his desire for her threatens his plans.

Scarlett Delacroix believes she's sinned beyond forgiveness. So she accepts Raiden's offer of temporary passion as her last chance with him. Then she becomes pregnant. But she and her baby have no place in Raiden's future—unless he walks away from all he's ever wanted…

Don't miss the first exciting title from Olivia Gates's *The Billionaires of Black Castle:*

FROM ENEMY'S DAUGHTER TO EXPECTANT BRIDE

Available wherever books and ebooks are sold.